CONFLICTUS

Part 1
The Chronicles of the Light Princess

Kristen Dovnik

This book is for

my sister Lauren and my mother Cindy.

Because let's face it, if it weren't for your kick-ass edits
the world would never know the story of Kyra and Duncan.

Prologue

Looking at myself in the mirror. *Oh Zagoria, I look like crap.* My eyes are glassy and sunken in from yet another crappy night sleep. My dreams filled with all the horrors of the underworld, of the battles that I know I have yet to fight. The visions that never cease to end. But they will, they have too, I cannot let them win.

Taking a deep breath, I splash some water on my face and head out the door for my morning run. It's a beautiful crisp morning here in Sydney and the birds are chirping as the sun begins to rise. The sun, my oldest companion, without it, life as we know it would cease to be. The world would perish in a blanket of darkness and despair. However, I am getting ahead of myself. I should tell you where my story really begins.

My name is Kyra Reynolds and I am the Light Princess. To anyone who crosses my path, I would look no older than mid-twenties but I am actually 347 years old. I am one of only a hand full of people in the universe who are immortal. I was not born of this realm. I am from a realm called Zagoria. An invisible world on top of the one you see every day. Zagoria is the realm of the ancients. Most of us who are from there have a divine purpose, a pure reason of being.

I was created to protect the sun, the light basically. *You are probably thinking why was she created to protect the sun?* Well, you see there is someone else in my world, a person created not for good but evil, someone known as the Dark Prince. He wishes to destroy the sun and in doing so, creating complete and utter darkness. Unleashing all sorts of unspeakable horrors into the world. Creatures that are too vile to speak of.

It has been an endless battle between us for centuries. We don't age and are technically classed as immortal beings but we can still die. Just in a different way than humans do.

An immortal blade forged of fire can kill an immortal being and lucky for me, I actually have one. Many creatures from the fiery depths can kill us too but thankfully we defeated their kind many millennia ago. The difference between us and humans, is that when myself or the Dark Prince die, we get reborn with a clean slate, a fresh start. No memories passed down and no clues on how to take down our enemies. Absolutely nothing!!! I've even been told that every time we are reborn, we don't even look the same. Even the Dark Prince, so until he shows his face, we don't know what he looks like in this lifetime. Only his past selves. Which makes it really difficult when we are trying to find him. I only know all this because of our Elders. They were created with all the knowledge and provide all the teachings and training that Zagorian's, myself and the Dark Prince need throughout our lifetimes. They hold our history. It is only because of them that I know any of this. When the Dark Prince or I die and are then reborn with no memories of the past or our former selves, it is our Elders who teach us. They are here to help us understand our two worlds. They know everything. You could say they are like our very own Google search engine....

The Dark Prince and I rule over the two halves of Zagoria, everything the light touches is mine and all that lies within the darkness is his. *Even those creepy dark passageways? Yep, you guessed it, all his. Ergghh !!*

Growing up, I was always told that I am a Princess and though there is no higher rank than mine, I have never really felt like royalty. I sure haven't been trained to be royal. Since the moment I could walk, I have been trained to kill and eliminate all vile creatures that the Dark Prince sends my way. I was trained in hand to hand combat from the age of 4 and gun training and weaponry by the age of 7. The title Princess has never sat well with me, I feel more like a warrior than a Princess. I am someone who doesn't mind getting their hands dirty. I am most certainly not built for frilly dresses and a crown upon my head.

I have known all my life that this is what I was designed to do but I must hide in today's society as no human can know who or what I really am. When I was a youngling, I never understood the reasoning behind why the elders warned me not to show the people who I was. I remember thinking that I was a higher being, like some sort of goddess to them. Someone that they could trust and come to in times of need. Someone like the old Egyptian gods or something. But as I moved through the ages, I became aware that some humans aren't very nice. They see anything strange to them as a threat. I have seen beings from other worlds come here, only to be taken away to some far-off government facility and experimented on. That is not how they are supposed to treat visitors, they should be creating allies, not enemies. However, sadly that is just how some humans are.

As an immortal, I have to regularly move, find a new and different place every couple of years. I don't want people noticing that I am not actually ageing. Even though I have the ability to use mind control if I wanted to, it is just easier for me to move on and find a new place. I live my life as normal as I can, getting jobs and living in domestic apartments or houses. At first, I found it quite difficult to stay undercover, nonetheless, I have it down to a fine art now. Understanding the risk of exposure is a good motivator to make sure that I do not draw attention to myself. I did try a few centuries ago to change my appearance and the minds of the locals, so I could stay in London a little bit longer, unfortunately though it didn't work out, people started to notice in the end so I had to leave anyway. I find it hard sometimes to leave, especially when I fall in love with the place and its people.

The Darkness however, is creation's worst enemy but with my help humans will never even know it exists. The Dark Prince who controls the darkness will stop at nothing until he is the one in control of the earth's surface and I, I will do everything in my power to protect it.

In all the years I have lived I have never come across the Dark Prince. He has never shown his face, choosing to always send his minions to do his bidding for him instead.

He sends them in an attempt to take me out, forgetting that they are not strong enough to take me on but still he tries anyway. It doesn't matter how much I try and torment them to give up the location of their master, they never budge. They are loyal to him through and through. His minions are the ones that help instil fear into the minds of humans. The great depression, wars, self-pity, lack of confidence, among many other things, these are all creations of the Dark Prince. Without this fear, he cannot survive. So, you see my life is anything but normal.

Chapter 1

Today I'm not thinking of any of that, I'm thinking about the mountains of paperwork that I need to get done, new order forms and invoices for the crew, and payroll forms that need to be filled out and delivered. The list is pretty much endless. This job sometimes feels never-ending. I could summon a minion to help me but that would essentially blow my cover, so I'll just cover my scowl and get to work. I am the assistant for the CEO of a small construction company in the heart of Sydney. It is nothing too fancy, but that's the point. Just what I needed to help me with my disguise. I need something where I can leave at any moment and no one will notice. It's not like I couldn't change their mind if I wanted to but I try not to if I don't have to. With humans, it scrambles their brains a little if I use my powers on them too often, I learnt that the hard way back in 1764.

Reading through the invoices for today, it looks like we have a huge delivery of material coming sometime this morning. Lots of gyprock and villaboard by the looks of it. This will make the guys happy as last week's delivery was missing a lot of material and it pushed our progress back by a few days. Nonetheless, with this delivery we should be able to get back on track and hopefully finish the job on time.

Standing up from my corner cubicle, I decide I'm going to need a lot of coffee if I am going to make it through this day alive. Walking over to our little kitchenette, I see Felicity, our accountant, standing there eating her breakfast. She smiles at me between bites. Trying to cover her mouth while saying "Morning," with a mouth full of food. *Charming Flick, real charming.*

"Morning Flick, how was the date last night with the Hotty?" I ask giggling. Flick has been going on and on for weeks saying how much she wants to date one of the guys out on the site. Finally, last week she got up enough courage to ask him out and then acted surprised when he actually said yes. Turns out he wanted to ask her out too but was too afraid of rejection or something. *Who knew?* Mind you, Flick looks like a damn Victoria Secret model, all long legs, sexy hips, voluptuous bust and volumes of thick, coffee coloured hair on top of her head. No wonder he was too intimidated to say anything to her, most people are usually drooling over her when she speaks to them. Flick, on the other hand, is as shy as a mouse. It takes a lot of guts for Flick to do pretty much anything.

"Oh my gosh, Kyra he was amazing! He took me to the little Italian restaurant down by the harbour, you know the one I have been dreaming about going to? We had the best spaghetti bolognese that I have ever tasted. I'm not kidding, you should totally try it. It was amazing, then when the cheque came, he paid for everything, even though I told him

I'm paying because I was the one who asked him out. He didn't want to hear it." She paused to giggle like a little schoolgirl. "Then after dinner, we went for a walk along the water and he held my hand. OMG Kyra, he is amazing! I honestly think I'm in love. He was so sweet and charming and well come on, you've seen him, he is just so damn sexy".

"Hahaha, well actually no, I don't think I have seen him, there are heaps of guys who work here, so he could be anyone, however it does sound like you had a great time. This guy sounds nice, just don't go getting all mushy straight away. I don't want to see you get your heartbroken again." Last year Flick was dating this guy, everything was working out great, until one day the man's wife rocked up at the office and blew every door in Flick's heart wide open. It took her months to get back to her normal self.

"Did I hear someone went on a date?" questioned Connor, our boss, as he walks through the door.

"I did and it was amazing," Flick says gushing like she is in love, with the biggest grin on her face.

"Oh really? Do I know the guy?" He moves past me to make himself a coffee, trying his best not to look directly at Flick. You see, if I were a normal person I wouldn't be able to notice how jealous Connor is of Flicks date. But it is because I am not normal that I am able to notice his pheromone levels, they give him away. His anger spiked, then disappeared as quick as it came. Everyone else in the room is completely oblivious to his reactions, but not me, Connor has feelings for Flick. I sensed it the first time I saw them together. I have always wondered why he's never asked her out.

My senses are sometimes that strong I can pick up any changes in emotions and pheromone levels from within a fifty-metre proximity. It's annoying that I can't switch it off, then again it comes in handy when I can sense someone or something around me that shouldn't be there, like when a disciple of the Dark Prince is present.

"Yeah, he's one of your guys out on the site," says Flick.

"Oh! Which one?" Connor asks trying to hide his hurt.

"Come on Connor, do you really want to know?" He thinks about this for a second, looking a little lost, then shakes his head as if to say no.

"Nah it's alright. I'm better off not knowing anyway." Flick gives him a shy smile expressing that yes, it is better him not knowing and while turning to make herself a coffee her phone starts ringing as if on cue.

"Oh crap, I'll see you later guys." She says while quickly stirring her coffee, throwing her leftover toast in the bin and rushing back to her desk. I smile after her, she makes the days working here so much more enjoyable. Connor, on the other hand, seems a little sad. He is in his late thirties, has dark brown hair that's cut pretty short and has devilish light blue eyes that most girls would die for. He is tall framed, roughly six feet tall, slender but also quite built. He is a good-looking guy and deserves to be happy. I can see how much it pains him to watch Flick talk about all the dates she goes on and I see how lonely that makes him feel. He just hasn't found the right women yet. She is out there though, I'm sure of it. Realising I'm just staring at him, I mentally shake myself. *It's time to get the day started.*

"Hey, I was looking at the invoices for this morning and it looks like we have a huge delivery of material arriving around nine forty-five, should I go let the guys know or do you want to do it yourself?" I ask while grabbing myself a cup of coffee. Taking a sip, I sigh deeply. *Oh! that's good.*

"Ah crap, I have the meeting with the board of directors this morning remember? Can you run out there and tell them?" Downing his last mouthful of coffee, he returns his cup to the coffee machine and makes himself some more. Looks like he may have a big day ahead of him too.

"I thought that meeting was tomorrow?"

"Nah, they rang me this morning to change it. I sent you an email earlier about the change. They want the progress reports and with the lack of materials we've had over the past few days, I don't have much to give them. They've been breathing down my neck since the beginning of this project and honestly, I don't give a shit. We will finish when we finish, there is only so much I can do. At least if materials are coming in today, we might still be able to finish this job on time." Grabbing my phone out of my pocket, I load up my emails and sure enough, there is one there from Connor that arrived at five am. *I should have checked my inbox on the train.*

"Fingers crossed...Should I just let Brice know or all the foremans?"

"Umm, Brice is fine, he'll let the other guys know when it's in. Oh! And tell him that they need to move the excavator out of the way so that the truck will be able to park on-site this time. I don't want it out on the street like last time. I am sick of copping all the fines." Shaking his head, he walks off towards his office. He's probably remembering the last time the councilwomen popped in to deliver the fine personally.

"OK no problem, I'll tell them." I state laughing because I know Connor hates it when the council pop around. Especially when it's old lady Sally. She is a constant flirt and only ever tries to seduce him. Poor Connor, she would almost be twice his age but that doesn't stop her from trying to ask him out.

Back at my desk, I switch out of my heels, put on my steel-capped boots and grab my hi-vis vest and hard hat out of the drawer. No-one is allowed outside during production without them. I swipe the delivery form from the printer as I head out the door towards the loading dock.

There are probably around twelve hundred workers on this current job and all of them work in this blistering heat. Australia's weather is harsh sometimes. It is roughly thirty-four degrees out here today but with the sun belting down, it feels way hotter. I feel sorry for all the workers inside the building. With the sun hitting those windows and not much ventilation, it must be pretty unbearable to have to endure.

We are currently working on a building that will house nine hundred and sixty-seven new luxurious rooms for some fancy hotel here in the heart of Darling Harbour. With a view like this, I bet they will charge a fair bit of coin for them but then again, this is Sydney and everything here is expensive.

I work on the ground level in one of these little shipping containers that we use as offices on some job sites. We have a central office, but it is quite a distance away and Connor likes us to be close to the job, so these are what we bring in and use. Lucky for us though, we have air conditioning. Unlike the building site.

Being here makes our job so much easier, especially when we need to get a hold of a foreman who refuses to answer their phone. Plus the view, that really is an added bonus. We can see all the high rises in the city. All the windows glistening with beautiful, vibrant, reflective colours. It looks magnificent. We can see the eye tower, Sydney's tallest building and all the boats coming in and out of the harbour. The shining blue water looks so nice and inviting that you just want to go swimming in it. Even though the air is hot, it smells so divine with all the food shops along the water beginning to open and preparing for the day ahead.

I see Brice about hundred metres to my left, conversing with the forklift driver. Something must have been funny as I see them both throw their heads back in laughter. Wiping the tears from his eyes, he sees me approaching, so he says his goodbyes and closes the gap between us.

"Morning Kyra, what can I do for you on this fine morning?" he asks smiling and fiddles with the traffic paddle in his hands.

Brice is always so happy to see me. He has been with the company for only a year now but he has become more than a worker to me. He feels more like family. If I were to have a grandfather, he would be the kind of man I would hope my grandfather would be like. He is in his sixties with a love for his family and his friends. He treats everyone with kindness and is always willing to listen when you need someone to talk to. He had been trying to get a job for years but unfortunately because of his age no one would risk hiring him but I did. The age thing maybe a little worrying but I found him to be as fit as a fiddle. Nothing stopping him from taking on a job such as this. He's loyal, never late and is extremely hard-working and that is what we need on a site like this. Someone who we can rely on.

"Good morning Brice, you're looking well today, how are you feeling?" Brice had been a little under the weather for the past few days but lucky for him it was nothing more than the common cold.

"Thank you, my dear, I'm feeling much better."

"That's good"

"What can I do for you missy?"

"Connor wanted me to inform you of a delivery which should be here in roughly thirty minutes. He also wants the guys to move the excavator so that the truck has space to park this time please. He doesn't want to get another fine like last time." Chuckling as I give him a shy smile. I know that the boys did not mean to forget last time, it was just a very busy day. But still, the look on Connors face when he got the fine was priceless. I believe he was reacting more to the provocative outfit Sally chose to wear that day, rather than the fine.

"Sure, thing sweetheart, I'll get the guys right on it" Grabbing his two-way radio to inform the men about moving the machine.

"Awesome thanks, here is the delivery form, please make sure the driver signs it this time, ok?" Crossing my arms, I give him a commanding look. He always takes delivery of the materials correctly but forgets about the paperwork.

"Sure, love, I'll try not to forget this time. Is there anything else I can do for you or is that it?" He asks as some loud bang happens above us making us jerk our heads up in its direction.

"I'm... I'm pretty sure that's it for now, thanks" I say as I slowly bring my head back down, looking at him again.

"OK, I'll bring this back to you later Kyra" Holding up the form for emphasis as he starts to walk off.

"Thanks, I'll see you later then" I say as I turn around and start walking back towards the office.

You can hear people way up high, laughing at something that they thought was funny. One of them, their laughter is so hilarious, it reminds me of a donkey. I can't help but shake my head and smile as I walk along the path. *Oh, I love working here.* I can hear throngs of tourists milling around the harbour and I don't blame them, it's such a beautiful day to go sightseeing. Sydney is such a delightful city to explore, wishing I was out there with them instead of sorting out paperwork all day. *But oh well.* I dream to have an office outside, somewhere where I could soak up as much sun as I could. My powers grow stronger with every bit of sun I get, it helps me fight off the constant attacks that are sent my way.

Walking back to the office, I start to get the strangest feeling, as if something is not quite right. Like I'm being watched or something, and yes people do look at me all the time but this feels different, bad kind of different. The hairs on my arms begin to rise and I have a feeling I know what's coming. *Darkness!* Nausea rises in my throat before I smell the stench of hatred coming my way, filling my nostrils. Quickly, I walk towards the wide-open space in the middle of the holding bay, this way I will be able to judge exactly where the creature is before zoning out. A few people are walking around but everyone is too busy to notice me. *Good, that's what I like.* Slowing my pace, I quickly grab out my phone, pretending to make a call.

Putting the phone to my ear, I stop walking and look around. I am unable to see anything but I can feel it. I must locate the being before it attacks me here in the open while I'm unprepared and still in the human realm. I should conjure up a weapon but I can't, I must not blow my cover. The dark creatures are invisible to the humans but sometimes they can sense when they are around but most of the time people believe it is a ghost or a supernatural being, so pretty much they are right. Others just feel a chill run down their spine like something is not quite right. The creatures are vicious monsters that mainly like to lurk in the shadows, feeding off the human's fear, however, some like to do more than that to humans.

Fortunately for me, I can see them but on a down-side, they can attack me while I'm still in the human realm. If there are people around me, it would look like I'm fighting nothing but thin air. Making me look insane and I hate it when people think I'm crazy. It has happened once before, only the once and I swore then that I would never let that happen again.

I need to fade out, hopefully I still have time. I just need to locate it first. *Where are you?* I can feel the darkness consuming the air around me. *Crap! I'm running out of time. I need cover and I need it fast.* Looking around I notice a shed with its doors wide open to the far right, thinking fast, I start walking towards it. As soon as I'm inside, I fade out, switching realms and automatically back into my true form. The only beings that will be able to see me now are the ones from here, my home, my Zagoria. I'm now invisible to the human's, however, to the Zagorians, I look like the sun. My blonde wavy hair has turned into a glowing fire on top of my head, bouncing and flickering in the light breeze, making my neon green eyes stand out even more. My golden and white armour has beautiful intricate Celtic swirls that wrap themselves around my entire figure, knee-high shiny steel boots with the gloves to match. A picture of a gold sun lies solely on my stomach and in my right hand, I conjure up my sun sword. My immortal blade, the hilt has the same sun design that is on my stomach but the blade, it is made of pure fire and lightning. Ready to kill anything with just one swipe. The blade is smooth and swift and can cut through anything like butter. It's the perfect weapon to take on any darkness.

Walking out of the shed and back into the holding bay, I can feel the minion, it is maybe a hundred feet away but I'm unable to locate it. Holding my blade up, I turn in a few slow circles. Still, nothing, closing my eyes, I focus on my senses. *Oh, man! We have a stinker.* The smell coming from this thing is putrid, like wet dog mixed with rotten flesh. *It's disgusting.* Sensing its hatred coming from my left, I slowly turn in that direction, with my eyes still closed, I hear it move. Hear the scraps of claws hitting the ground. They seem to be getting faster. *Crap! It's coming towards me.* Quickly opening my eyes, I brace myself for the attack. Startled for a split second when I realise what is coming towards me. *I thought they were all but extinct. I haven't seen one of these in centuries, the last time I took one on was more than three hundred years ago... A Cerberus. One of the Dark Princes most loyal guard dogs but what is it doing here?* A massive dog-like creature standing at least seven feet tall with three ferocious heads. All snarling and drooling at me as it makes its way towards me.

I have a few seconds to prepare myself for the impact, knowing exactly how to kill this thing. Aim for the heart, not the heads. Positioning my blade for the best attack and ready to strike. It's coming at me fast, all four legs moving at crazy speeds, nonetheless, it underestimates how fast I am. Swinging my blade, I slice through its thick fur on the left side of its chest, cutting off only a slice of its hide. *Damn! I missed the heart.* It makes a slight screaming noise as it continues to run past me. Green blood starts oozing from the gaping wound. The smell is putrid but I don't let that distract me. *I must take it down.* The hound whimpers for only a second before turning around and heads straight back towards me, gaining more speed than before. Bracing myself, I get ready for the attack, aiming my blade once more, I know I won't miss this time.

The beast's faces are so close that I can feel its breath on my face as I hit my mark, dead centre, piercing its heart. Even with the blade in its chest, the hound's heads continue to attack but to no avail, as death starts to take hold, everything begins to slow right down. The heads become heavy on its shoulders and everything begins to sway to the side before crashing limply to the ground. After a few aftershocks and twitches, the beast goes still. Its lifeless body just lays there while I stare at it with astonishment. *I thought we got rid of all of them years ago in Egypt, how did this one slip by us?* Twenty seconds later, the beast evaporates into a puff of green smoke, this happens to every minion once it has been killed. Their souls are going back to the underworld, to his Highness, where they will swirl in the river of souls for all eternity.

Looking around I make sure there isn't any other being before I go back to the shed. I need to get back into Earth's realm before anyone realises I'm gone. It's not rare that they attack me here at work but it still doesn't change the fact that I'm surrounded by mortals who always like to question any weird behaviour. I just try to do my best so no one notices when I disappear. Darting quickly inside, I make sure that I'm still alone before I fade in. The ripple happens so quickly, like a shimmer in the light. Once I'm back on Earth, I grab out my phone, putting it to my ear and pretend that I was on the phone this whole time.

"Sure thing, I'll get that to you right away....... Ok, thanks, have a great day" I speak to the phone as I walk out of the shed, before pretending to hang up and slipping the phone back into my pocket. I don't think anyone noticed what I was doing. Which is always a good thing, I'd hate it if I had to try and explain why I was taking a phone call in the shed, especially when my office is roughly two hundred feet away.

Once I'm seated back at my desk. I get a text from Brice.

Delivery has arrived. Everything going well. I'll let you know when it's done. Brice

Sending a quick thank you back, I put down my phone and get back to work. I love it when deliveries go well, means less stress for Connor, which means less stress for me.

Chapter 2

There is one thing about Connor that not many people know. He is a lover of food. Especially fast food. Greasy goodness that he loves to lick straight off his fingers. Which is why he is always extremely happy when lunchtime comes around, I swear that man just loves to eat.

"Hey, Kyra?" Connor calls out from his office.

"Yeah?" I shout back and then quickly decide I should get up and head in there.

"Could you be a darlin' and please go get me something for lunch?" *Why am I not surprised?* Three out of five days I work here he gets me to buy his lunch for him. The other days he usually just gets me to warm up his leftovers from the night before. I don't mind though, at least I can go outside and soak up some sun while I'm at it. I am feeling a little drained from the encounter earlier with the minion anyway.

"Sure thing, what would you like today?" Knowing it will be probably anything greasy and most definitely deep-fried. A little while ago he told me to get him whatever I thought was good. So, I came back with salad wraps. He wasn't ecstatic over the healthier option but he ate them regardless. Even if he bitched and moaned the whole time.

"Hmm, I don't know, surprise me." *Seriously? has this man learnt nothing?*

"Are you sure you want me to do that?" I give him a questioning look, knowing exactly what I'd like to do if he doesn't tell me what he wants. *I hate having to pick for him.* It's very hard to buy junk food for a man who doesn't like eating the same thing twice in a fortnightly period.

"Ah, on second thought maybe a burger or something, just none of that healthy crap you like ok? You know I'm not a fan of salads" he replies smiling.

I stand there smiling back at him, he knows full well that I would have gone to Healthy Soul or something like that and bought him a salad. The man eats way too much junk food but who am I to judge, if that's what he likes, then that's what he'll get.

"Sure, thing boss, greasy food coming right up." I reply, as I turn and walk towards the door.

"Ha-ha, very funny thanks, darlin."

The food market isn't far from the site so I decide to go there to buy our lunches. I grab Connor a chicken combo deal knowing that it's his favourite, and before leaving I stop and grab myself an on-the-go sandwich from the deli stall. They always make the best sandwiches.

While walking back, I see Flick standing near the entrance talking to a guy in our uniform. I'm guessing that's her date from last night, her body language definitely implies that it is. *And wow she wasn't kidding, the guy's hot, like smoking hot. Man! Why isn't he a model?* He is at least six foot five, no six foot six and has black shaggy hair that hangs over these intense cyan blue eyes. He has a strong jawline that could cut right through paper like a razor. Even though his body is slender, he has these massive arms that are trying to bust out of his work shirt. *Like seriously, get a bigger shirt before you tear this one.* He looks like a Greek god or what I think a Greek god should look like in human form. *Damn! That was her date? Seriously? He's gorgeous!* He flicks his eyes in my direction and I duck my head. *Shit! He saw me staring!* I feel another set of eyes on me and I try to pick up my pace.

"Oh, hey Kyra, come here! I want you to meet someone," Flick shouts and waves me over. *Too late, she saw me!*

"Oh hey..." I yell back, trying to act like I didn't see them standing there. I walk over, even though I should go straight back to the office with Connors food. *At least now I'll have an excuse to leave.* I feel his eyes upon me the whole time, like he is burning a hole in the side of my face.

"Kyra, this is Duncan, Duncan this is Kyra, she's the friend I was telling you about," she states looking at Duncan as he stands there with his eyes focused on my face. *What is up with that?*

"Oh cool, nice to meet you." He says with this smooth deep voice trying to sound nonchalant, I feel anxiety radiating off him. Perhaps Flick makes him nervous.

Wouldn't surprise me as she has her body almost completely pressed up against his.

"I hope what she's told you about me was all the good stuff." I duck my head chuckling. "But it's nice to meet you too Duncan," I utter as I extend my hand out for him to shake. Without a second thought, he puts his hand in mine.

I'm instantly hit with this full- body rush of energy, an alien feeling that pushes all the air from my body. Electricity has ignited from where we are touching, the sensation feels like love and warmth and safety. Like Duncan is my anchor and I'm a floating balloon above the surface of the earth. Making everything feel right, future battles can be won as long as we stick together. I want to live in this moment forever and never let go... *WAIT! NO! STOP!*

This is too intense I must let go. Dropping his hand abruptly, I stare at the space between us. Catching my breath and regaining my control, I look up at the both of them. Duncan looks like he is in a daze staring at me and in that moment I know that whatever just happened, he felt it too. I can see the questioning look in his eyes. *Sorry buddy, I have no clue what just happened.* Taking a deep breath, I risk a glance at Flick, slightly freaking out that she just witnessed whatever that was. Thankfully though it appears she didn't see it. She's still staring at Duncan with so much love and affection in her eyes, like she's too love-struck to notice anything. *Phew!*

Shaking my head to rid it of the remnants of the sensation, I decide now is the best time to leave.

"Sorry for the quick intro and run guys, but I have to go and take Connor his lunch," I exclaim, as I hold up the paper bag containing Connors, probably cold chicken.

"It's was nice meeting you Duncan... I'll see you back in the office Flick," I utter over my shoulder, as I turn away quickly, hurrying back to my office.

I have to physically force myself to focus on work for the rest of the day. Keeping my mind busy is the only thing I can do right now because if I don't, as soon as I have a single second to think I keep drifting back to Duncan. Those dreamy blue eyes, his sexy smirk and the shocked expression on his face after we touched. He knew that I felt the same sensation that he did, he saw it on my face when he looked at me. In all the years I've been alive, I have never felt anything like that before. It is completely foreign to me. I don't even know where to begin if I had to try and explain it to anyone. *I should consult the elders; they might know what the hell that was! Who is he? What is he? Is he human? Maybe he's not human, maybe he is from Zagoria? Nah surely, he can't be. But then again, I haven't met all my subjects, so maybe he could be. What if he is from there? That's a good thing then, isn't it? What does this all mean?*

Get a grip, Kyra! Stop thinking about him. He is Flick's and that is that. But the way he smiled when I went up to him, the way his cologne smelt. He smelt so good. His hand felt so perfect in mine when we touched... *ARGH! THAT'S*

IT NO MORE! I can't deal with this any longer. I'm going to see the elders tonight and that's final.

Three thirty rolls around and it's time to go home. I send off the last statements to the workers and contractors and shut down my computer for the day. I have to check everything twice to make sure I haven't forgotten anything because the universe knows I can't think straight right now. I stand up from my chair, push it under my desk and turn around to grab my jacket and bag from the hanger, then head for the door.

"See you tomorrow Kyra." Flicks calls from her cubical as I head out.

"Yeah sure, I'll see you then" I call over my shoulder. Grabbing out my phone to check for any messages. SMACK! My head rams right into someone's hard shoulder. *Ouch!* Trying to regain my balance I realise it was Connor's shoulder, the impact causes him to drop his clipboard, resulting in a loud bang as it hits the ground.

"Oh crap, sorry Connor I didn't see you." Feeling foolish, I bend down to pick it up.

"It's ok Kyra, how's your head? You hit my shoulder pretty hard." he replies trying hard not to laugh as he accepts his clipboard.

"Yeah sorry about that, my heads fine though, thanks. I kind of got distracted." Holding up my phone to emphasize my point. He nods in agreement while crossing his arms.

"It's all good, you leaving?" he smiles down at me.

"Yeah, I left you a little note on your desk with your schedule for tomorrow, however now that I've caught you, I might as well just tell you now. You have another breakfast meeting at six am tomorrow with the board and a toolbox meeting with the guys at nine in the lunchroom on level three. Also, Paul and Stan, the tiling contractors want to have a word with you sometime tomorrow too, not sure why but they asked if you could send them a text with a time. That's all I think you have for now, though I'm sure more things will pop up throughout the day."

"Okay awesome, and thanks for today Kyra, I'll see you tomorrow." he steps aside to let me pass.

"See you tomorrow," I say as I walk past and head towards the train station.

It takes me a full hour to get home from the city. I don't mind taking the train though because honestly, I would rather this than being stuck in the afternoon traffic. I live in a huge, old two-story Victorian style home south-west of Sydney. It has these beautiful red bricks with a black roof, cream coloured gutters and railings and a full wrap-around porch. My garden is in full bloom consisting of lilies, frangipanis, orchards and peonies. Everything smells so divine, it's wonderful and inviting, just the way I like it. I love the area where I live too, it's much nicer than living in the claustrophobic CBD.

A few years ago, I used to live in the heart of Sydney. I got sick of all the hustle and bustle so I decided to shift further south and I have never regretted my decision at all, it's the best thing I ever did. Here it's so quiet and peaceful and I can protect my perimeter better against the constant attacks from the Dark minions. They occur almost every night. Most of the time it's only one creature, but lately there have been times when it's been more than one. *I don't even break a sweat.*

I drop my bag by the front door and set my keys in their usual bowl. Walking through the foyer I head towards the staircase. *I need to get out of these clothes.* I quickly go upstairs and into my bedroom and go straight to my walk-in wardrobe. Once inside I just stand there for a few minutes trying to think of what I should wear. It's not going to matter once I switch realms so, sweatpants and a singlet will do just fine. No one is going to see me in them anyway. After changing, I go back downstairs and grab an apple off the counter. I'm not hungry but I need to keep my energy up, so I guess this will do just fine. Eating it quickly, I then throw the remains in the bin and look around my kitchen. I guess it's time, I need to see Elder Willow. I cannot wait any longer, hopefully she'll know what is going on with me.

Moving to my living room I fade out. Changing back into my true form I blink a few times to help my eyes adjust to the sudden brightness that now swarms around me. Sometimes I wish I could alter my appearance while I'm here so I'm not walking around like a giant lightbulb, but at least I can put my sword away, otherwise that would be really annoying.

Zagoria is such a beautiful place, it looks just like the surface of the earth except for everything here seems to have a purple shimmery tinge to it. This is my home and although I have no parents or siblings, no family at all for that matter. There are a handful of selected elders that live here who were chosen to raise me, and to me, they are my family. *Even when they get on my nerves.* I have no blood relatives because I was not born by a mother but created by a force however, I love the family I have chosen unconditionally.

I walk through the front door of my Zagorian home and into my garden. The stars shine brighter here, making my garden glow with greenish, purple lights. I could sit here for hours just staring at all the beautiful flowers, I miss it when I have to switch back. To the far side of my garden stands a little replica of my house, a home that I built for my girls here in Zagoria. Lucy, Daisy and Pixie are my good luck charms and also my border protectors. They are fairies who stand no more than twenty centimetres tall and they help to create the protective barrier that lies solely around the perimeter of my home. If they were to ever leave, the barrier would collapse and my home would no longer be my safe haven. Their magic works in both realms, keeping it protected and no one can enter the property without my permission. If permission isn't granted, the girls alter their minds and make them believe they have already been and are now leaving. It's quite fascinating to see in action.

"Good evening ladies, how are we?" I say smiling down at them as I walk over.

"Oh Princess we are wonderful, how are you?" They all say in unison. Lucy, Daisy and Pixie share the same brain. When I was a youngling it really freaked me out but now I find it as normal as waking up in the morning. They have been with me for nearly three hundred years, ever since I moved out of Willow's place. They were her parting gift to me as she could no longer keep me safe herself.

"I'm good, about to head over to Willows, any trouble today?"

"No creatures today Your Highness," they all say smiling.

"Awesome, thanks ladies, I'll be back soon ok? See you later." I wave to them as I begin to walk away.

"See you soon miss." they utter, then scurry back into their house.

They are so sweet but they don't like to talk very much. It doesn't bother me though, because neither do I.

Heading out my front gate I see Zagorian's walking about, there are so many of them. They all stop to bow their heads as I walk past and it unnerves me, all the formalities and stuffiness, it's something that I've never felt comfortable with.

Chapter 3

Willow only lives ten blocks away so I decide to walk. She lives in an old run-down, white fibro home on the corner of one of the busiest streets in all of Zagoria. The house looks like it could fall apart at any second but I know she won't move, no matter how much I try and beg her. She loves her old home. It's the house that I was brought up in. Its walls hold all those memories from a lifetime ago. *Well, what feels like a lifetime ago anyway.*

I walk up to the front door and knock six times with a three-second break in between each knock. Willow is a little strange sometimes and won't open the door, no matter how many times you knock. I learnt years ago that if I used a special knock sequence, she will know for sure it's me and come open the door. It works ninety per cent of the time.

She opens the door slightly, popping her head out just far enough to see if I am alone. Her old age has made her slightly paranoid. Lifting my hand I give her a little wave and she smirks and opens the door wider. Quickly she grabs my arm and yanks me over the threshold, slamming it shut behind us. She pulled me in so fast I almost tripped on the skirting as I moved through the doorway. Don't let Willow's appearance fool you, she may look like a little, frail old woman but she has the strength and stamina of an elite athlete. Standing about five foot two she has long grey hair that is always braided down her back and she wears these big square glasses that are too big for her face. It makes me laugh sometimes watching her push her glasses back up onto her nose. I wonder why she has never gotten a new pair. I'm sure I could find an optometrist if she needed one. I'm certain it would make her life easier, not having to fix her glasses all the time.

Willow pulls me in for a hug. I try to resist as I don't like to be touched but knowing it's been a while since I saw her last, I let her have it. She's what I picture any mother or grandmother should be like, sweet, caring, loving and generous. *Just minus the paranoia.* She has gotten worse over the past century and I don't have the heart to ask her why. If it was really important, she would tell me.

"Your Highness, it's so kind of you to drop by, what do I owe this pleasure?" She questions while curtsying before me. She loves to play this game when I don't pop over for our monthly visits, likes to pretend that she doesn't even know me.

"Come on Willow it hasn't been that long. Besides, when did you start calling me Your Highness again? It's usually something like Princess brat or Princess pain in the ass but never Your Highness."

"Oh, but it's who you are sweetie and I am not above the law, you know that." Mocking me as she shakes her pointed finger at me. "Princess pain in the ass does suit you better though, I must agree." *Much better.* Looking around the room I notice not much has changed. She may have removed a few ornaments from the mantel but other than that it's all relatively the same. The couches are worn with age and the rug has definitely seen better days. House plants are scattered everywhere throughout her living room, taking up nearly all the floor space. I am amazed that she can still walk around considering all the clutter. I have always wanted to redecorate her house for her but I know she would never allow it, so I just drop the subject.

"Alright fine but aren't you glad to see me? What has it been, like five months?" I'm a bad somewhat daughter, I really should come by and visit her way more often. Considering we live so close and I did move out here originally to be closer to her.

She glares at me for a moment before shaking her head.

"Five months? Try more like six since you decided to show that beautiful face of yours around here, and yes I am very glad to see you." She walks over to her normal chair, sitting down and putting her feet up on the footrest. "Come now child take a seat... have a drink, I made your favourite" *Of course she did.* Willow can sense when things are going to happen, so she probably knew I was coming.

I take my seat opposite her and grab a glass of her freshly squeezed orange juice. Putting the glass to my lips I take a sip. *Mmm, that's so good!* "I don't know how you do it Willow but this stuff is always amazing!"

"Thank you sweetie, now tell me what is on your mind?"

Taking a deep breath I relay it all to her, recounting all the events that led me to come here. The touch, the power, all of it. "I've been going out of my mind all afternoon thinking about it. Honestly it makes me feel like I'm going crazy." I murmur while putting my head in my hands. *How did I let myself get so worked up over this?*

Willow sits there in deep thought, tapping her fingers against her lips. Her facial expressions prove that she may, in fact know something. By the looks of it she is deciding just how much she is willing to disclose. *Great. Please don't tell me it's going to be another half-answered response.*

When I was a youngling I approached Willow with a question, a question that I knew only she had the answer to. *How did the last Princess die?* I found out years prior that I had a predecessor. It's not something that the Elders like you to find out about until after your initial training but I did, I just never found out what happened to her.

One night I gave up trying to study her death in the papers that were scattered around my house and decided to approach the one person I knew who actually knew her, Willow. "What happened to the last Princess?" I asked, walking up to her big chair in the corner of the living room and taking a seat on the floor at her feet. "You know I can't disclose anything about that, it's in the past and you know its forbidden." *Which is correct, it is forbidden even though I have no idea why.* **"Please Willow? ... I have to know, just tell me... please .... I promise I won't tell anyone you told me." I had**

given her the biggest pouty face I could muster and to my astonishment, she caved. Throwing her hands up in the air she said exasperatedly, "Alright! Fine I'll tell you but you need to swear that what I am about to tell you never leaves this room, got it?" She had stared me down, giving me a pointed look.

"Scouts honour!" I had giggled as I put two fingers to my chest declaring to all that I wouldn't tell. I had scooched closer so I wouldn't miss anything and Willow had shaken her head smiling as she leaned back in her chair.

A sad smile had crossed her face as she began to speak. "Her Highness was elegant and full of grace just like yourself, she was a true beauty to behold. Nevertheless, we believe the Dark creatures perceived her as too great a threat to the Dark Prince. On the last night of her life, the creatures of the dark massacred the Princess's guards and attacked the Princess by the hundreds.

To this day we still have no idea how they managed to get through the barrier. She had been completely outnumbered, there was no hope of survival. We had no warning of what was occurring until you appeared in the parlour. I'm not sure how they managed to get around my ability but they did and us Elders have never seen such an uprising like that one before. Unfortunately she was unprepared and lost the battle."

I remember that night like it was yesterday. I cried myself to sleep over the loss of the Princess. Willow wouldn't elaborate on exactly how the previous Princess died, only that she was seriously outnumbered and didn't survive. Due to being reborn and having my memory wiped clean I didn't retain the memory of her death. The elders are unsure as to why it happens but this is why they are here, to help guide us towards the right path. They help by filling in all the gaps that we are missing. I've never been told why we are not allowed to know about our past predecessors but I have a feeling it's because they are afraid of the repercussions of us knowing, that it might cause us to fear certain situations. I've been instructed to go into all fights without any fear. Fear is a weakness, a weakness the darkness can exploit.

Willow gives me a strange look. "Why do you think this boy has affected you so?" I sit there for a moment thinking about the question.

"That's the thing Willow I don't know, I've never been affected by a male like this before. This is all new, the sensation is powerful. Is this normal? Does this sort of thing happen to everyone? Can you not beat around the bush this time and help me understand what is happening?... Please? I'm so confused." I say showing my defeat. I hate not knowing what is happening, especially when it has something to do with me.

"Ok, I'll try to explain this the best I can. You see this sort of phenomenon doesn't just happen out of the blue, it is a celestial power that connects you to another, a power within two people connecting to make a whole. This sort of power cannot be detected by humans, only beings with magical traits can feel it. As you are one of the most powerful beings in our realm you feel everything more strongly but I need to ask you, this boy, was he oblivious to the power you felt or did he feel it too?" She asks me curiously.

Duncan's face pops into my mind "He felt it too, I'm sure of it. If what you're saying is true though, then wouldn't that mean he's not human? That he could be one of us? But if he is, how was he able to elude my senses?" *If he was able to feel the power, that means he must be one of us and if so, how was I not able to detect any power within him?*

"Us Zagorians have the ability to do many great things but hiding who we are is not one of them. Having said that, if you truly believe he felt it too, that can only mean that he is a Zagorian. Maybe you were blindsided by this man's true identity because of your attraction to him. I can't be certain that this was the case because I wasn't there.

This power I speak of has the ability to mess with your mind, your emotions and your decisions. It makes you second guess yourself about everything, what is right and what is wrong. It's guiding you to one thing and one thing only. Tell me where your mind wanders off too."

I give her the 'what do you think?' look and reply "Of course I'm thinking about him, it doesn't help we are talking about him though, he has been on my mind all afternoon. It doesn't matter what I do I can't stop myself from thinking about him and I've tried almost everything." Taking a deep breath in and out before I continue. "I still don't get all of this Willow, what is this power and why do I feel so strongly for a guy that I just met today? It doesn't make any sense to me."

"Kyra you feel so deeply for this boy because he is your other half, he is yin to your yang, your partner in crime, your forever songbird. This boy whether you like it or not will share your life from here on out...What I'm getting at Kyra is you feel so strongly for him because he is and forever will be your soulmate."

All the air leaves my lungs making me feel like I can't breathe. *She's joking, she has to be. This isn't real. But the pull, I can feel it even now, so what she's saying must be true.* "Soulmate?" I ask in complete and utter shock, slouching back in my seat as if I've been punched. *What does she mean by soulmate? I can't have a soulmate! Because if it's true, then what she said to me when I was younger can't be accurate...* Sitting up quickly I argue, "Wait, what about all those years ago when you were training me," pointing at her, "you said that love was evil, that loving someone was a distraction. A distraction someone like me can't afford. Now you're telling me that I have a SOULMATE, how can this be true?"

"Sweetie love is a distraction, love makes people blind and they could potentially end up neglecting their duties. We never wanted that to happen to you, you know your duties are too important. You need to protect the earth from the darkness. You've known this truth your whole life, it's your destiny. Nonetheless, even a Zagorian Princess can't avoid fate. You and this boy were destined to meet. You are soulmates and that means that your souls were searching for each other, you just didn't know it.

But I must warn you, now that you've touched, it will be torturous to stay away from one another. Being a Zagorian means you feel emotions more deeply than any other species and your souls will now yearn and fight to draw you back together. You must fight the urge to be with him though Kyra, for the sake of the world. Don't let your guard down and don't get distracted. We don't want what happened to the last Princess happening to you." She stares at me with her big eyes.

I know what she means, my predecessor died because she let her guard down and paid the price, it shook the elders to their core. It's frightening thinking about what happened, so many creatures all attacking her at once. She was unprepared for an attack that size but then again, I don't think all the preparation in the world could have saved her.

"I understand it's my job to protect humanity but how am I supposed to do that now if my body is being pulled towards the one thing that is too dangerous to have? If my destiny is to protect the humans, against all these odds and without any distractions then why did fate do this to me? Why did it give me this monumental distraction?" I look at her sadly. Fate can be so cruel sometimes. Suddenly feeling very overwhelmed, I just want to cry. My body wants him so badly, I can feel my heart calling for him. I want to be with him but my responsibilities must come first.

Protecting the humans against the darkness, that's what I need to focus on. *Fate will have to wait... but I feel that's going to be easier said than done I'm afraid.*

"Sweetie it's just the way things have to be. The humans need you; you know that you can't let yourself get distracted, you just can't. I don't even want to think about the consequences if you do. If you let this boy into your life anymore than you already have it could be highly dangerous for everyone. Not just for yourself but for the humans and the Zagorians too. Your bond will make you fight to protect him and only him. You will put his needs first and you cannot let that happen. Our worlds depend on you Kyra, you understand that?"

"Yes of course I understand, it's what I have trained my whole life for. My duties must come first... always." I nod agreeing to everything she has said. Sadness washes over me. I hate that she is right, I must stay away from Duncan. Maybe once this is all over, then and only then will I allow myself to love.

"I'm so sorry this happened to you Sweetie. Especially at a time like this. I have been told we are close to finding the Prince's location, so we need to focus on that right now... Never in my wildest dreams did I believe that fate would draw you such a bad hand but it is what it is. You will have to live with and learn to fight the constant pull towards this boy. Fight the urges to be with him. It's not going to be easy. Frankly, it's going to be excruciatingly hard. You are a strong and powerful woman but this fight is going to much different. Just think of this as another obstacle that you need to hurdle. You can achieve anything you put your mind to. We all believe in you, you just need to believe in yourself too."

Gosh, I love this woman, she's right. He is just another boulder in my path, something I'll be able to manoeuvre with ease. I can do this. I know I can and I know what I must do. Taking a few deep calming breaths. *Relax Kyra.* I need to think more clearly before I say anything else. Willow is right, my reason for being needs to come before anything else. It's what I was made to do, no distractions ever, those are the rules. They have been imprinted into my brain from the moment I took my first breath. That's the deal and I have always acknowledged it.

I can already feel that it's going to be hard to stay away from him, my body is being pulled to him even though I have no clue where he is. I bet if I was to follow the pull I'd find him, he would wrap his big, strong arms around me and hold me close. *Damn it! Focus Kyra!* As Willow said, he is an urge I must fight, will fight! Humanity is more important than me having a love life right now. That's why I barely even have a social life, it's too distracting. I'll consider a love life after I take down the Prince but for now, NO DUNCAN!

Sitting up straight, I take one more deep breath.

"You know what Willow? I agree, no distractions. My duty comes above everything else. Even if we are destined to be together I will fight the urge to be with him, the humans need me to remain focused on the task at hand. They need me to find the darkness and destroy it. Once we all agree that the humans are safe and this war is over, then and only then shall I allow Duncan into my life. I will stay away from him." I can feel it's going to be hard, this pull is way stronger than I originally thought but I've taken on tougher battles than this before. I'll just have to keep my mind busy with other things. Taking another deep breath, I hold it for a moment before releasing it. *I can do this!*

Willow is looking at me with a sceptical expression on her face. I bet she is deciding whether or not to believe me. I don't mind either way, I know my job and I will not let Duncan get in the way of that. Conquering the darkness is my only priority.

"Thank you Willow, your guidance is always appreciated but I better be going. Hopefully, it won't be another six months before I pop over and see you." Smirking as I get up and head for the door. I need to clear my head, even if I understood everything that was said I still need a little more time to process it.

"I'm not holding my breath... Keep your chin up Sweetie, everything will be ok in the end. Just keep doing what you've always done and you'll be fine. I believe in you, always have and always will." She gets up too and walks with me to the door. She rests her hand on my back knowing full well that I need a little comfort before leaving.

"I'll see you soon Willow. I promise." Turning to my left I give her a swift kiss on the cheek before walking out the door and into the cold night air. She doesn't say anything, just curtsies and closes the door. Shaking my head, I smile in her wake. *Silly old woman.* I love her to bits but the whole formality thing drives me insane. I know I am the 'Princess' but to me it's just a title, one that I can't remove no matter how much I've tried.

Don't get me wrong I love what I do. I love having a purpose, it's just that I hate this formal stuff. Like I hate my birthdays, even though I live in a different realm I still have to come back here every year for my birthday without question. The elders hold a huge party in my honour. A party where the whole kingdom is invited and when I say everyone, I mean everyone.

My birthday is also a day of truce. One thing that I have always thought strange is that the Prince and I share a birthday. That means we were both reborn on the same day. I've asked the Elders several times about how that came to be but as usual they wouldn't say. It's either to protect me or they don't even know themselves. Nonetheless it's something that always has me wondering. Our predecessors died on the same day and I'm curious as to how the Prince died. *Because if the Princess didn't kill him, who or what did?*

Anyway, due to our shared birthdays, it's a day of truce and all the dark creatures of the underworld partake in the festivities. As for the Prince himself, well no, he never celebrates or attends. He still won't show his face or reveal himself. Even on his birthday. It's the only day of the year where there is to be no conflict, a twenty four hour non fighting period. It's one of the oldest bylaws we have in

Zagoria and we may only have four laws, but they are absolute and binding.

These rules consist of:

1. The Prince and Princess are the highest ranks in the realm.

2. The Prince and Princess's birthdays are to be a day of truce.

3. Fighting is not permitted within 50-yards of any Zagorian elders property.

4. No creatures Dark or Light are allowed on the surface of the Earth without being summoned by the Prince or Princess or the approval from the Elder council first.

Breaking any of these laws is strictly forbidden and punishable by death.

Chapter 4

Walking back towards my house I decided that I might as well go and check on the Order of Light while I'm here. The order consists of over three thousand Zagorians who risk their lives every day to help protect the humans. These are ordinary Zagorians who made the ultimate decision to protect. Believing that my purpose is just they volunteered their lives to help fight against the darkness.

Over a hundred years ago I was propositioned by a group of thirty or so Zagorian men and women who wanted to do whatever they could to assist me in conquering the Dark Prince. They believed that the Prince was growing stronger every day and they wanted to see what they could do to help stop him.

At first, I was unsure as to how they could help me so I did the only thing I could think of and I took them to see Willow. Willow in return sent us to see Elder Kit, a seemingly young elder who has a great deal of knowledge in combat training. He taught these Zagorians all they needed to know and then individually tasked them in areas where their skills would be of the most benefit to aiding our cause. While overseeing a training session one day he came up with a truly marvellous idea and put out a proposition to see if any more civilians wanted to join. Within a month he had more than nine hundred new recruits and from that point on it grew to be what it is today.

Three blocks further down from Willow's house resides an old aeroplane hanger. We may not use aeroplanes in our realm but the humans surely do. Hence why this is here, the planes however are not but that is irrelevant. In the human world I have seen to it that this hanger is no longer in use. Back in the nineteen hundreds when the order was first starting out there was speculation that the hanger was haunted in the human realm. With the high traffic of Zagorians moving in and out of the hanger the humans became wary and afraid and no longer wanted to go anywhere near it. With the hanger not being used there was a high risk of it being torn down so I decided to purchase it off the council. Claiming that I wanted to utilise the space for storage. They were a little sceptical but they didn't deny me, I guess they were just happy to see it sold.

The hanger is large enough that it can hold up to four Airbus A380's and still have plenty of space to move around freely. It's now our official Order of the Light headquarters. They eat, sleep and train at the compound, making sure they are all available for whenever the alarm for help may sound. At the far end of the hanger are the rooms that were constructed to house all the soldiers. Next to them is a huge obstacle course set up to look like the streets of Sydney. As roughly seventy-five per cent of all attacks lately are in the city, it's beneficial for the troops to get used to the layout. There are multiple things to manoeuvre around, climb up on and jump over which allows them to create plenty of strategies to take down the beast as quickly and as efficiently as possible.

To the left of the obstacle course is the lunch station, this is operated by the husbands and wives of the soldiers. Some of them live here but most of them only come here to help out. And lastly, on the right side near the entrance of the hanger is our command post, the area run by our commander and chief, Elder Kit. I can't be here as often as I would like, so I delegated command of the order to him. I prefer it that way too as he was the one who started the order and trained them, they all respect his command. They are loyal to the cause and him and I will be forever grateful for what they are doing to help stop the spread of darkness. The Prince won't win because as a team we won't let him.

As I walk through the entrance of the hanger it's as if time stops. Everyone in the room stops moving and talking and in unison they all turn and stare at the glowing ball of light standing in their doorway. I really dislike that my appearance causes this reaction whenever I enter a room, it's eerie having everyone's eyes on me. Looking around the room I notice that every single pair of eyes are on me except one, Elder Kits. He is preoccupied with all the papers scattered on the table. I shriek and launch forward as the door slams shut behind me, causing a loud bang in the quiet room. Kit snaps his head in my direction looking as if he may tell me off before realising it's me. He quickly regains his composure, straightens his tie and clears his throat.

"Your Highness." He proclaims, as he bows before me. All at once everyone else remembers who I am. Following suit, they all bow or curtsy as well.

"Elder Kit, everyone, it's so nice to see you all again." I give everyone a quick wave as I make my way over to the command post. With the formalities out of the way everyone goes back to what they were doing before, the entire hanger is suddenly engulfed with so much noise that it makes it hard to think. Warriors groan as they make their way through the obstacle course, women are laughing over something that was said and pots and pans crash as they are moved throughout the kitchen. Everything is so alive; I'm honoured and so proud of what we have achieved here.

"Good evening Your Highness what a pleasant surprise, it's been a while since you came to visit. How have you been?" He leans in close kissing me on the check. Elder Kit is the only one I don't fight on the formalities; he has told me time and time again that he will never drop it no matter how much I ask. So, it's better to play along than waste my breath.

"I've been alright, nothing really out of the ordinary. Looks like everyone here is doing well too and by the looks of this it looks like we are impacting the Darkness more than I thought." I gesture towards the map of Australia on the wall with pins all over it. There would have to be thousands upon thousands of different coloured pins on the map. Every time we take down a minion we put a new pin on the board. The Elders learnt throughout the millennia's that the Prince's minions like to follow him around like flies, surrounding him, creating masses which eventually evolve into nests. Nests are usually a clear sign that the Prince has been in that area for more than a few days, he could still be there or has already moved on. Either way, we track the nest and their patterns, hoping that one day it will lead us to him.

Around thirty years ago our scouts found that the numbers of creatures congregating here in Sydney was increasing substantially. The masses growing so much in such a short period of time, could only mean one thing. The Prince was here. So, I packed up my life in Paris and moved to Australia. We have been trying to trace his exact location ever since. I have a feeling we are getting close. *We must be.* I have been killing creatures on the daily now. Sometimes one, maybe two, occasionally even three, but those are just my numbers. The soldiers go out in the masses and takedown hundreds. *We have to be getting close.*

"Yes, this week alone we have taken down two nests of Crawlers in the south, a nest of Haunters in the north and at least three hundred creatures scattered throughout Sydney. That brings our total to one thousand three hundred and sixty creatures killed just this week alone," he declares proudly. He is as devoted to his troops as they are to him, caring for them like they are his children. I'm glad to see him so happy, nonetheless he is always happy when we have a kill list as high as this one.

"That's fantastic! However, I am pretty sure the total is one thousand three hundred and ninety-four. I too, have killed a few since my last update." I respond smirking, knowing full well that he will like these numbers.

"Outstanding!" Grabbing a handful of pins from the tray he walks over to the map. "Locations?" he asks without even looking at me.

"Twenty-four were taken down at work, seven at my house and three outside central station." I give him a big grin; that's a good number of kills for only six days. It doesn't beat the record though as the highest number of kills in just one week goes to Damon Steel, he managed to take down fifty-six beings within four days. I remember being here the day he came back after we all assumed he was dead. He was all bloodied and bruised, limping his way through the hanger door. Some of his wounds were so horrific that we thought for sure he was a goner. Thankfully though we have the best healers in all Zagoria volunteering here at the hanger. Against the odds, they managed to bring him back from the brink of death.

He and five others had gone out in search of a nest that was reported south of Gage. The nest was allegedly only a handful of critters and could easily be taken down by the six men but when they got there, the nest was way bigger than anyone could have expected. Encountering numbers way higher than the initial report, Damon told us that all the men fought their hardest but perished quickly once the creatures realised they were there. There would have been at least seventy Crawlers in the hive and Damon took most of them down by himself. We didn't hear from them for four days and we presumed them all dead. We were gearing up to send in more troops when he came through the door. His story is now one of legend, even though it did only happen ninety years ago.

"Great work Your Highness, I bet there was barely a struggle on your behalf as always. However, with the increasing numbers around your work I insist that we increase your personal detail, especially around the harbour. I have no doubt you can handle your own but it would give us Elders peace of mind knowing that you had a little extra protection around you." He stares at the new pins on the map with a concerned look on his face. *Here we go again.*

"Kit, I understand the reason for concern and yes I'm more than capable of defending myself but increasing the numbers is unnecessary." I hate when he tries to up the security, they just stand there staring at the job site for hours on end. There are far more important things that they could be doing with their time.

"Your Highness, your safety is our number one priority, without you the Dark Prince wins and if he wins what we're doing here is all for nothing. Please just let us do our job by protecting you." He turns to face me head-on and judging by his stance he will not back down on this matter. *Sorry Elder, neither will I. I will not have them risk their lives to protect me when I am more powerful than a group of them put together.*

"Kit I know you want to protect me but I would rather the warriors out there fighting the Darkness, not watching the job site. What they are all doing is amazing and I don't need any more protection, I can handle it."

"We all know that Kyra but your workplace is not safe, you are not safe there anymore. If you won't quit then let me do this for you, it will help me sleep better at night."

"I'm not safe anywhere, the creatures are naturally attracted to me and you're right I won't quit."

"Fine just let me send, I don't know, ten more soldiers."

"No." I declare shaking my head.

"Please Your Highness just ten more that's it, I promise."

"No." I announce as I feel my temper rising.

"Your Highness, it's for your protection."

"I said no." I feel as if I am about to explode.

"Please just..."

"ENOUGH KIT!" I bellow and the noise around us begins to dim. "You already have twenty-five guards at the site as it is. I said I don't need them and I won't allow you to send anymore, twenty-five is already too many. I let it slide before but not this time, I know you mean well and I understand your concern but I'm fine. You trained me well in my youth and I am more than capable of killing these minions on my own, trust in me." I give him a stern look that says 'don't push it'. I hate it when I have to use my authority over the elders, I love them all dearly, however when they try to ram what they want down my throat I can't stand it.

Giving me a sad expression as he shakes his head Kit turns away from me and ponders over the map once more. *I hope he's abandoned the idea.* Everyone starts to continue with their activities once more and the noise resumes. Taking a deep breath I walk over to the desk to check the stats on the computer. I need to familiarize myself with where the attacks have been mostly occurring.

Scrolling through the statistics it turns out that Darling Harbour is the spot that gets attacked the most. There seem to be no nests but the singular attacks are getting worse by the day and right around where I work too. *Wow, they are drawn to me!* In the last seven weeks the number of attacks around this area has increased by a total of nineteen percent, at least twelve beings are killed their daily. *Is that why he wants to increase my security? Why didn't he just say so?* Turning my head I look out towards all the Zagorians in the compound. *Do they know how bad it's getting out there? Do they realise there is a rise in attacks?* Elder Kit surely must've told someone else. *If he is so afraid for my wellbeing, why didn't he just tell me about this during our argument? I hadn't realised it had gotten this bad. I still probably wouldn't have agreed to extra security but it would have explained his insistence and it would have been nice to know.*

Lost in the spreadsheet before me I barely notice the commotion at the entrance to the hanger. The noises and voices get so loud it encourages me to investigate. I turn my head just in time to see Damon barrelling through the throngs of people gathering around, his sword is still drawn and covered in what I can only presume is demon blood. He must have been in such a rush to get here that he didn't even have time to put it away let alone clean it off.

Damon is a beast to behold standing around seven feet tall with massive shoulders and arms that could seriously rival tree trunks. His sandy blonde hair looks a little odd upon his head as it doesn't match the rich colour of his skin. To any Earthling he would probably resemble a bodybuilding surfer, he is the warrior of legend. The man who took on many and has a killer story to tell about it. Glancing around the room he spots Elder Kit and runs towards him. A man on a mission he doesn't notice me as he runs past the desk. *Oh my he smells disgusting, a clear sign that he has been fighting, but where?*

"Commander Kit I've brought back all the wounded I could manage but we are going to need more soldiers. The nest in Dellpond is growing out of control and we are losing men left, right and centre. Those of us who managed to escape did and are waiting in a safe location until back up arrives Sir," he announces with shortness to his breath. From the way he is huffing and puffing, he sounds as if he ran all the way here from Dellpond. I jump to my feet feeling the need to make myself useful. I will go with them; they will need my help to take this nest down. *They are my people and fighting for our survival after all.*

"You may have all the troops you seek Damon but may I ask, how big is this nest if fifty soldiers were unable to take it down? Exactly what creatures are we up against this time?" Kit speaks briskly as he walks over to the training area, getting ready to make the announcement.

"I believe it's the three-headed dogs of old Sir... The Cerberus... We've been under the impression they've been extinct for years but I'm certain that's what they are, Sir." Damon says the with as much courage as he can muster. These creatures obviously scare him, I can see it. *So I was right, something is terribly wrong, especially now if there is a nest of them. How are there so many? I thought the Prince only had a handful of them.* We were certain that we got rid of all of them over three hundred years ago but now they have been sighted twice in one day. *What's going on?*

"Cerberus's?" Elder Kit stops walking, turns around and stares, clearly gobsmacked.

"Yes sir I believe it is them, almost certain."

"But no one has seen one of them in years, how is this even possible?" Kit's face turns a full shade of white. I guess he is having the same thoughts as myself. If the hounds have come back, what else could be out there? I'm scared to imagine. I shudder at the thought. *There are worse things out there than a Cerberus.*

"I have." I blurt out.

"What?... When?" He turns to me giving me an even more shocked expression.

"At the job site... Today."

"But how can this be? Why am I only finding out about this now? Didn't you think it would be vital for me to know if a creature as strong as this one was roaming around again?" He looks at me with wide eyes, he's scared and I don't blame him. The Cerberus almost wiped us out the last time we fought; we were lucky back then. Hopefully, this time is better.

"Sorry, it slipped my mind." I say guiltily. *Oops.*

"How can they be back? We destroyed them years ago," Elder Kit utters under his breath not directing it at anyone.

"What if we didn't Kit, what if we only thought we did? Maybe they wanted us to believe we destroyed them all, that way we would be unprepared for an attack like this one."

"It would've been nearly impossible for the Dark Prince to hide them from us for so long. Think about it Your Highness, it has been over three-hundred years and this is the first time we are hearing about them again." He has a point, there is no way we wouldn't have come across at least one before now, considering the size of this nest. It just doesn't seem plausible.

"You're right it's nearly impossible for him to hide anything from us these days, especially a horde of beings as great as this. We did kill them to extinction and once a beast is dead that's it, it's dead, it can't come back...unless." Whipping my head to the right I look over at the bookshelf, the books containing our history. The stories of the Prince and all his domains. "Oh I hope I'm wrong," I whisper as I turn back to face them. "If they are back, I believe it could only mean one thing and if my suspicions are correct then we are in for a world of pain. The only way a beast can come back is if there are problems with the river of souls. It could be the only explanation to why they are here. Once a beast is killed, they usually can't come back and you said it Kit, the Prince couldn't have hidden them from us for over three hundred years." I declare, looking at them both. I watch as they both finally grasp what I'm trying to say.

"What do you mean by problems? We were never taught about anything like this occurring. Can this be true Commander?" Damon pipes up swinging his head from side to side, trying to look at the both of us in turn, waiting to see if we will have the answers he requires.

"I'm sorry son, unfortunately I don't have the answers you seek, not this time." Elder Kit looks gravely at the floor lost in thought. My worst fear has come to fruition, even an elder doesn't know what is going on. *Looks like it will be up to all of us to find the answers.*

"What do you mean commander? What is happening?" Seeing as Kit doesn't have the information he seeks, Damon now looks at me for answers. I don't know exactly what is going on but I'll tell him what I think it might be, something that I have been pondering over since I saw the Cerberus this morning.

"Damon, we were never taught about the river of souls ever having any issues. It's supposed to stand there as our beacon of hope. For us to believe that these beasts can be killed and never return but I think they have returned.

Which is terrifying. I think the river is collapsing, it's the only thing I can think of as to why they are here.

If you remember during your training, once a beast is killed its body dies, trapping it in the river for all of eternity. There is no possible way for the beast to come back but it appears they have and if the Cerebus are here, I dread to think about what else may have come out too. The river is the only thing protecting this world from the creatures and if they get loose, then we are no longer safe. Earth is in danger and I have a feeling lots of people are going to get hurt before we figure out how to stop what's coming."

Chapter 5

"Danger, what do you mean by danger? We were taught to believe that as long as you are alive we are all safe. You're the guardian of the light, the only thing standing in the way of the Darkness. Why can't you stop whatever's happening?" he asks me confused.

"Damon please understand my predecessors and I have been dealing with this conflict for centuries and killed countless of beings. Some creatures aren't even known to us anymore as the records only go back so far. Yes, I may be the guardian of the light, the protector of the sun and I fight the darkness as that is what I was created to do but this... This is new and I have no idea how to fight this. It goes beyond even my training.

If I'm right about this though, then all the creatures that we have ever killed will be coming for us. Thousands upon thousands of them and there is not enough of us to take them down alone. We will need more recruits, way more if we are to even stand a chance against them." *Shit! Recruits!* I got so side-tracked I completely forgot about the group of troops waiting for backup. I look towards Elder Kit but he is still staring at the floor, lost in thought.

"Kit! The soldiers, they need our help! We have been distracted by our conversation that we forgot to send help...

Elder Kit?... Hello?... Can you hear me?" He is so deep in thought I don't think he even registers I am talking to him, he ignores me and continues to stare at the floor. "I said the soldiers need our help Kit. We must go! ARE YOU LISTENING?" I scream at him but he still doesn't look up. *Screw this, the others need us and I will not sit by and let them go in alone.* Leaving the command post I walk over to the training area. I have everyone's attention due to my little outburst at the commander so I announce,

"Ladies and Gentlemen we have an urgent situation. We received a message from our brothers and sisters out in the field. They are battling a nest of Cerberus, the three headed hound of old and require our immediate assistance. For those of you who are willing to fight please gear up, we leave in 5 minutes." Turning back to the Elder I see he is so struck by our conversation that he hasn't moved from the position I left him in. He is in no shape to lead right now as he looks as if he might faint, he's gone as pale as a ghost, what we discussed has completely rattled him to the bone.

Damon on the other hand is leaning against the desk staring at all the troops moving in and out of the hanger. I'm getting the impression that the information no longer concerns him. *Why does he look so happy suddenly?* Disregarding Damon for the time being I walk over to Elder Kit. Taking his arm I lead him over to the couch, he doesn't say a word or even try to stop me as I make him sit down. I ask one of the wives in the kitchen to look after him while I'm gone and if she has any trouble, I tell her to call Elder Fox, he will know what to do.

Making my way outside I see at least two hundred people piling into trucks. Everyone is moving at lightning speed; they look like blurry figures whizzing around the place. Walking up to the first truck I see I jump into the passenger seat, within thirty seconds our convoy is on the move. It's a short drive to the riverfront in Dellpond but it seems like forever, anxiety and anticipation are coming off the soldiers in waves. Everyone is on edge, geared up and ready to go. *We can do this!.*

As we are getting closer to the river I decide to conjure up my sword, you never know when something might jump out and I may need it. My sword lights up the entire cabin and I quickly drop it to the floor. I don't want it distracting Benny anymore than it already has. He looks over at me and I whisper "Sorry," feeling bad for momentarily blinding him while he's driving. He shakes his head, smiling before turning his head back to look at the road.

We arrive at the riverside apartment building where Damon instructed. It looks relatively new, nineteen levels above ground and possibly two or three below. The building is quite large and looks like it has many places to hide. *Great! Looks like we might have our work cut out for us.* It's eerie quiet, you wouldn't think that anything was going on inside however, we know differently. I can feel their hatred radiating through the stone walls and let's not forget about that stench. That smell is a dead giveaway, the odour is so bad that you can almost taste it, it's foul. I thought the one Cerberus smelt bad but this, there must be hundreds in there. Getting out of the truck I walk towards the large group of people awaiting further instructions. The troops that called for back-up have come out of hiding and joined our ranks. There is a considerable number of us now, hopefully it will be enough. *It's time to bring the pain.*

"Alright people gather around; we have confirmation that the creatures are inside this building and according to my senses there would have to be at least a hundred that occupy this premises. Most of you would never have dealt with a Cerberus before, so listen up. First things first, do not and I will repeat, do not aim for their heads. This will do absolutely nothing. You must aim for the heart; the heart is the quickest way to kill them. It's on the left-hand side of their chest, directly under the left neck. Their skin is ridiculously thick and covered in fur, it's very hard to penetrate so be prepared as you might not get it on the first try.

You must not let this creature get on top of you either, this gives it the perfect position to strike. The heads are ferocious and will stop at nothing until you are dead. If the creature somehow ends up on top of you the quickest way to get rid of it is by kicking it in between the legs." There are a few chuckles from the women within the group, but the men just have a smug look on their faces. *Well, it is known to be the quickest way.* "Most hounds in our history have been reported to be male, so this is a pretty safe manoeuvre to implement to get yourself out of the situation. Has anyone got any questions about the hounds?" Looking out at the group before me I see most of them shaking their heads, fully understanding what I said. During their training they were briefly taught about the Cerberus, I made sure that all the creatures of old were included in their lessons even if they were extinct. *Well were supposed to be.* They had to know just how bad some of these creatures were. Lucky for us we had the forethought to include these creatures in their lessons if they are all going to reappear.

"Alrighty then, let's begin, I want from this line here to the end to go around the far side of the building. Head on in and watch your backs people, these things pop up out of nowhere." I lift my left arm and pointing to what I believe is a third of the mass, gesture with my right arm back towards the building. The group breaks off and vanishes into the shadows.

"Now, from this line onwards I want you to break into two groups, one attacking from the left-hand side and the other from the right." Moving my arm a little bit more to left, I signal with my right arm back towards the building. Immediately they break off and do as instructed.

"For the rest of you, follow me, we are going in the front." I raise my sword high into the sky, letting everyone see it. Turning around I head towards the front door.

Roughly seventy of us make our way through the door and immediately I know that something is off. The foyer looks immaculate, there is a beautiful reception or security desk to the right-hand side of the entrance and on the left-hand side, I can only assume is what looks like a waiting area. It has a few couches, little coffee tables and magazines scattered everywhere. The creatures didn't come in this way or the whole place would be trashed. Seeing as there is nothing here we keep moving.

As we move throughout the foyer, the troops break off into little groups to do their security checks. My senses are going haywire due to the mass of creatures that must be congregating within this building. There is a pulsing beacon coming from below the ground, it feels as if a herd is moving around down there. *They must be below.* Resting my back against a wall I peer down the hallway and discover there are elevators and emergency exit stairs. *Bingo!* Waving my sword around I manage to get everyone's attention. Talking would be too risky so I decide to motion with my fingers instead. With two fingers together I shake my hand twice pointing towards the fire exit, then once at the floor. Getting the gist, they all nod and head for the exit.

I'm the last one through the door after I complete one last sweep of the foyer. The sounds hit me first. Downstairs the soldiers are screaming, terrified and tortured screams, maybe there is more down there than I originally thought. Looking down over the railing I see a Cerberus, it appears to be on top of one of our soldiers roughly three floors down. Its heads are in a flurry as it makes its attack. *Shit!* Sprinting down the stairs as quick as I can I rush towards the bottom level, I make it to the final landing and throw myself at the creature with my sword drawn. My blade makes a sickening slurping noise as it sinks into the beast's flesh, hitting its heart from behind. The critter sways a little before collapsing on top of the soldier.

Withdrawing my blade I jump down off the beast, moving around to its heads to get a better look at the fallen soldier. *Oh no, it's Benny.* Crouching down beside his head. I say a little prayer of thanks. "Thank you for your loyalty to the cause, thank you for wanting to find a way to end the darkness, thank you for being you, another beautiful soul lost to this terrible war."

Lifting my head I look through the open doors of the lower level into chaos. There are soldiers and creatures everywhere fighting, screaming and falling as death takes hold. The parking garage is painted with red and green blood, dead soldiers line the walls as anarchy erupts all around them. Only now do I notice the smell down here, it's so overwhelming that I fall to my knees next to Benny and heave up the entire contents of my stomach.

That's disgusting! Wiping my mouth with the back of my hand, I take a few deep breaths. *We can do this! I can do this!* I repeat this until I have control over myself once more. Taking one last deep breath I pick myself back up with my sword in tow and run into the room before me.

For a few moments everything is just a blur. My sword swings and slices through every creature I pass. Before I know it I've reached the other end of the room, out of breath my heart is racing erratically under my armour, it's beating so fast it hurts. Having no idea how many of them I just took down, I turn around and see all the creatures sprawled out on the floor before they vanish into a puff of green smoke. *7...8...9... 10. I took down ten!* Looking around the room I see soldiers swinging their swords or aiming a bow-and-arrow hitting their desired targets. Grunts of achievement as the soldiers kill their targets and the growls of the beasts that notice their brethren's demise can be heard around the room. I look on with amazement and I am so glad that I am not battling this one on my own.

Sensing movement to my right I swing my blade, slicing off the furthest Cerberus head from me, causing green blood to spray out all over the wall. This beast is massive, it's almost double my size. Its heads become more ferocious now that they are down to two, they look like rabid dogs frothing at the mouth and getting ready to strike. *This one might be a challenge.*

Without any warning both heads charge with their mouths wide open, I duck, except unfortunately I'm too slow. One of the creature's heads latches onto my right arm and bites down hard, piercing the flesh. Screaming out in pain I unintentionally drop my sword. The pain is unbearable, I begin to lose consciousness but I have no choice, I must take it down quickly before it kills me. Shaking my head I try to clear the fuzziness that is taking hold, but to no avail, it only makes it worse. The hound still has a firm grip on my arm, blood is gushing from the wound, but I won't let it stop me, I know what I must do.

Turning slightly towards the creature I swing my left arm and punch it right in the eye. It slightly loosens its jaw but not enough for it to release me. The other head decides to strike back in retaliation but I'm quicker, dodging its movements even though I'm held tight by the other head. Before the head holding me can tighten its jaw again I punch it repeatedly in the same eye as before. I feel a rush of cold air hit my wound as the beast lets go, moving away from me slightly to regain its equilibrium.

Quickly sliding forward I pick up my sword and shift underneath the beast before the heads have time to react. I shove my blade deep into the beasts' chest, killing it instantly. Quickly rolling to the left, I get out of the way of the falling creature, it misses me by less than an inch as it hits the ground with a thud. The heads lull to the side as the creature lays there lifeless. *11!* Struggling into a sitting position I brace myself against the wall. *Breathe Kyra, you need to breathe.*

The pain in my arm is excruciating and starting to throb, looking down all I see is blood. *I need something to cover it.* Reaching down I tear off some of the fabric that lies at my waist. With shaky fingers I manage to tie the torn fabric around my arm, using my teeth to help tighten the knot. *Hopefully, that will stop the bleeding.*

Returning my gaze to where the creature was lying just moments ago, green smoke is now all that is left. The devastating smell and the blood loss makes me feel faint; I try not to let it bother me. I need to get up, I need to help the others. I look up and around the room, its chaos, there is blood everywhere and I hear the screams of the soldiers as the Cerberus attack. There are definitely more creatures here than we originally expected. *There is no way that fifty warriors would have been able to take on this many alone.* We brought more than two hundred with us and I don't believe even these numbers will be enough. There is roughly seventy of us left but over fifty of them. *We will not win this through skill and strength, I need to do something. What can I do?*

Soldiers are dying quicker than we can take these things down. *Think Kyra think!... I have an idea! Even if it will take all the energy I have left, I must save them.* I call upon the power within me, disregarding the pain in my arm and only on the task at hand. Standing up I hold my sword in front of me, conjuring up all the power of the sun, letting it take over, I am ready to end this nightmare.

"Protect those who cannot fight, defend the light as it shines bright, the Darkness cannot win this fight. I am the Light Princess, the keeper of the sun, Earth's protector and there is no one more powerful than me." I burn like a ball of fire as I shout to be heard over the commotion. Within seconds light erupts from my being as pure as the sun. Bracing myself I take one last deep breath, letting the power take over. With power pulsing through my veins I shoot off into the mayhem around me like lightning, moving faster than the speed of sound. Taking down Cerberus after Cerberus, slicing and stabbing every beast that gets in my way. The beasts don't even have time to react before I take them down one by one. I'm moving so fast that even my comrade's eyes don't have time to adjust as I whizz past them. I'm fire and lightening, I am the sun. These creatures must die, not a single one can leave this building.

I have no idea how much time has passed when I collapse to my knees. It could have been minutes, hours, I just don't know. I'm physically drained after using so much power, I need to sit for a while and allow the built-up energy to leave my body. My senses are muted as I come down from my outburst. It's a strange sensation not being able to smell, see or hear anything. I'm not sure as to why it happens, all I know is there is nothing I can do to stop it. I just have to wait for it to pass.

As I begin to regain control of my senses I start to hear them, the soldiers. Some are confused with what they just witnessed and some are shocked, some are even scared but they all seem to be coming to the same conclusion. What they just witnessed, it won us this fight. I gained enough power to kill the remaining hell-hounds. I have to give credit to the power of the light, it's so dominant that it takes control of my entire being and does what needs to be done. The first time I used it when still a youngling, it scared the crap out of me. I never knew that kind of power ever existed and what scared me more was that I could wield it. I rarely use it though, it's highly dangerous for everyone if I am to die when that power has control over me. Again, the Elders never explained why, their only instruction was to use it in times of great need. They warned me that if the power is within me when I am killed the humans could be in peril as a result. I pushed and pushed for them to tell me more but as usual, I got nothing.

Regaining most of my self-control I stand up on shaky legs and look around the nearly empty room. All I see are dead bodies everywhere. I'm not sure how long I was sitting there waiting for my control to return but it appears it may have been a while. The soldiers are moving their fallen comrades and friends out of the room, taking them back to the trucks so we can give them a proper burial at the compound.

There is so much blood it covers every surface of this underground carpark. I'm in the middle of the room taking it all in, all the sadness, the anguish, I feel all of it. It saddens me deeply to feel this much pain. Peering to my right I see Damon kneeling over a fallen female soldier. He has tears in his eyes and is sniffling, sensing my eyes upon him, he looks up. His sorrow hits me like a bullet, raising my hand I place it over my heart, taking a deep breath, I wish I could take his pain away. He has so much pain inside for this fallen soldier, it's heartbreaking.

Returning his gaze to the women, he touches her face affectionately, swipes her hair off her wounded face and moves it behind her ear. It looks as if he is whispering things to her too; these are generally the actions of someone who has lost a loved one, then it hits me. *He did love her!* Most of us thought that Damon loved the fight too much to be able to love anything else. He is always so focused and dedicated to the cause and as far as we all knew he didn't have a partner. Perhaps he didn't, maybe his love was just never reciprocated, or maybe he never had the chance to tell her how he felt.

Is that what it would feel like if I lost Duncan? If by accident he was taken away from me before we got to know one another. I don't ever want to feel what Damon is feeling, I don't even want to think about it. I can't lose him, I won't! Wait! What am I thinking, stop it Kyra!

I pull myself from these thoughts and realise I'm staring. I stop myself and avert my gaze. I need to go help the others. I'm in such desperate need of sleep that I almost fall over when I take my first step. The sooner I go help, the quicker we can all go home and get some much needed rest. On the downside though, I have to get up in a few hours to go to work. *Great; Just great!*

Chapter 6

We are heading back to the compound with far fewer troops than what we set out with. I knew it was going to be bad as they had never dealt with hellhounds before but I didn't expect this loss. I'm dreading our arrival at the hanger. By far the worst part of my abilities is having to witness and feel the sadness and devastation from the families of the fallen soldiers. I've experienced it way too many times, it's the reason I despise war and it makes me feel dreadful that I lead one. However, we all know what must be done and why. We must win this war because if we don't then the darkness will take over and humanity will cease to be. We can't allow that to happen and I will try to spare them from as much pain and suffering as possible.

There are many days when I wish it was all over, that the Prince was dead and the Darkness gone forever. It doesn't matter what I wish for though because it will never happen, he would just be reborn like I was and it would start all over again. *THIS SHIT NEVER ENDS!* The fighting, this war, all the deaths, what's the point to all this fighting if there is no possible end, it makes no sense. A plus side to killing the Prince though, would be that while he is a youngling the dark creatures of the deep are forced to leave us alone until he comes of age. It may only be for eleven years but it would provide us with enough time to recollect ourselves.

Turning into the street of the compound I see people outside waiting with medical supplies, ready to tend to the wounded. I know I will need stitches as the wound on my arm just won't stop bleeding. I see the hopeful expressions on people's faces the closer we get; they are eager to see if their loved ones survived.

For many of them though it's not going to be a happy homecoming. I want to cower in the front of this truck and not have to face any of their pain but I can't. They all knew what might happen when they signed up but I still hate that they had to die for the cause. The families know that too and they know how I take losing people, especially like this. Don't get me wrong, I love that people are willing to stand with me and help fight for my cause but the deaths never get any easier.

We pull up at the hanger and start piling out of the trucks. Holding the doorframe tightly I try to get out but the pain in my right arm halts me from moving. Sitting back in my seat I take a few deep breaths. *How am I ever going to be able to get out of this truck? I feel like I'm about to faint. The pain is excruciating and I despise showing weakness.* A soldier who I don't know notices my struggle and rushes over.

"Here let me help you," he says as he reaches up and grabs me under the arms, lifting me up and out of the truck. I feel his arms flexing under my weight and his strong body sliding against mine as he lowers me to the ground. *Wow, he is muscular. Would Duncan's arms feel like this as he lifts me off the ground? Would it feel this good being this close to someone? Woah, Get a grip Kyra!*

"Um thank you for your help, I was struggling there," I say shyly to the guy in front of me.

"No problem Your Highness, is there anything else I can help you with?" he asks as he stands a little taller, belatedly remembering who I am. *They are always so intimidated by me.*

"Would you mind telling me your name, so I can thank you properly?"

"Oh, I'm sorry Your Highness, where are my manners? I'm Joshua." He extends his hand out towards me, I take it with my left hand and give it an awkward shake. He has huge hands. "Sorry Your Highness, I didn't see your arm." He moves slightly to the left to get a good look at the bandaged injury, blood runs down my arm onto the ground and he grimaces.

"That's ok, thanks very much for the help Joshua, much appreciated."

"You're welcome Your Highness, did you know you're still bleeding though? You need immediate medical assistance; may I take you to the infirmary, I can carry you if you like?" His happy expression changes into worry.

I feel embarrassed but I accept his offer, "Oh, yes please. I think I'm going to need stitches for this and I am starting to feel a little bit faint. I'm not sure I could make it there on my own." Peering down at my arm which is covered in blood, I see Joshua nod before he steps closer to me. He picks me up gently and starts walking us towards the hanger. As we walk I gaze at all the devastation around us. There are so many dead bodies, way too many for me to count. Starting to feel a little dizzy I rest my head on Joshua's shoulder, sensing the sudden change he begins to pick up his pace and as he does, everything goes black.

I wake up in a strange bed and I'm covered in wires that are connected to all types of machines, beeping noises are all around me and I'm having a hard time focusing on anything. *I believe I'm in the hanger's hospital wing.* As my focus starts to clear I notice it's a small room and made even smaller by the ten or so people in here with me. They are all talking in hushed tones. Not a single one of them has even noticed that I'm awake yet. I see their worried faces; feeling their fear before anyone has a chance to speak to me. *What are they so worried about, I'm alive aren't I?*

"Oh, thank Zagoria you're awake!... How are you feeling Your Highness?" Asks Elder Fox from the corner of the room. I didn't even notice he was here. He is the high medical Elder and has remedies to fix almost everything.

Slowly I sit up, stretching my arms and shoulders, feeling as if I have been hit by a truck. I'm sore from head to toe and my right arm is in pain, which reminds me of the Cerebus bite, I look down at my arm and it's covered in a bandage. I instantly start unravelling it, I need to see it. Shooting pain travels down my arm towards my fingers with the movement and I grind my teeth to prevent myself from crying out. I heal fast, maybe within a couple of hours or so but when it's a gaping wound it generally takes a little longer, so I usually just get it stitched up.

The last of the fabric falls away, turning my arm just slightly, I see what is causing me so much pain. The hound did a good job tearing up my arm, it's a complete mess. Nonetheless, the nurses have done a fantastic job at fixing me up but by the looks of it I haven't even started to heal yet, so I mustn't have been out for long. I look over at Elder Fox who has a worried expression on his face.

"Elder Fox how nice to see you. I'm a bit sore and a little disorientated but that's to be expected after the battle. When I'm feeling better, I will address our people and give a statement, if that's ok? I'm not quite up to it right now." I notice a few people in the room giving each other weird looks. *What's going on? Did I say something wrong?*

"Your Highness a statement won't be necessary, Damon has already given one to the people in your absence. It sounds as if you were all severely out-numbered out there. Thankfully a lot of you still managed to come back alive, thanks to you." He looks off into the distance for a moment before shaking his head, then returns his focus to me. "I must ask you Kyra, before you blacked out did you feel strange? Dizziness, nauseous, anything at all? Also, how long do you think you have been asleep for?"

"Um, I was in a lot of pain and began to feel dizzy. I can't remember if there was anything else. I think I blacked out pretty quickly once we got back. As for how long I've been asleep, maybe thirty minutes or so I think, why is that?"

"Your Highness, you have been asleep for almost thirteen hours. We were starting to worry that you wouldn't wake up." I am stunned into silence for a few seconds. *That can't be right.*

"Thirteen hours, how have I been asleep for that long?" I ask the room. *How did that happen, how could it? I barely sleep for an hour at night let alone thirteen!*

"We are not entirely sure Your Highness but we believe it may have something to do with the Cerberus bite. When you didn't wake up straight away we did a few tests, the nurses found high amounts of carbon monoxide in your system which may have caused the blackout. A few of the other soldiers who were bitten passed out as well, however none were out for as long as you were." Fox explains with concern lingering in his voice.

"Carbon monoxide? That's never happened, why now? We never experienced anything like this last time when we fought them." I'm confused, I have dealt with these creatures many times and they've never affected me like this. What has changed?

"We don't know why Your Highness, all we can do now is monitor your recovery and health. Do you feel dizzy, lightheaded or nauseous at all?" I move my head from side to side, back and forth, rolling my shoulders as I go.

"Honestly, I feel pretty good, my muscles and right arm are sore but otherwise I'm fine." I want to get up and out of this bed, I hate how everyone keeps staring at me. So, I have a little carbon monoxide poisoning, I'll heal, just like I always do. On the subject of healing, I look down at my damaged right arm and the resulting stitches. If I have been out for thirteen hours why haven't I healed yet? Elder Fox sees me staring and says,

"We are not sure why you haven't healed yet Your Highness, nurse Lexi stitched you up straight away when you were brought in. We thought the blood loss may have been the reason you passed out but upon further inspection, we realised it was the carbon monoxide in your system. Now that you are awake maybe it will kick start your healing abilities; we will just have to monitor it. I suspect you will want to get out of here as soon as possible, so the nurses just need to check your vitals one more time to make sure that you are ok and then you may leave if you wish."

I look back down at my arm. You better heal, I don't know how I will be able to explain this to everyone at work if you don't. SHIT! WORK!

"Ah crap, I missed work," I exclaim to the room as I put my head in my hands. I hate missing work. It doesn't happen very often but I don't do it as a rule. Days off result in people inquiring as to where I was. Somehow, I don't think telling people I spent my day off passed out in an old aeroplane hangars medical room with my arm ripped open is staying under the radar.

"I called your boss this morning and told him that you were ill today. He is such a nice man, I see why you like working for him," Elder Willow announces as she walks through the door into my wing, walking right past everyone else to get to me. Leaning forward she presses a kiss to my forehead before backing up and doing a curtsey. "How are you feeling Your Highness?" I roll my eyes at her formal greeting. Cheeky old woman.

"I feel fine, thank you Willow and thank you for calling Connor for me, I appreciate it."

"You're welcome Your Highness; we didn't want your boss to worry about you now, did we?" She smiles at me. I know they disapprove of me having a job, they don't want me to be working. They believe it's too much of a risk of being exposed but I like to keep busy, otherwise I'll go crazy sitting around all the time waiting for something to happen.

I give her a knowing smile, that's all I will be able to do at the moment with everyone in the room. When I am with a group of people, I must remember formalities. She used to reprimand me all the time in the early years as I wanted to be treated like everyone else. I still feel that way but I am older now and understand it is necessary.

"Good thing you called because he would worry. I was perfectly fine yesterday and then suddenly too sick to even come into work today? He's never known me to be sick, so thank you for calling him."

I look to Elder Fox. "Would your nurses be available to check my vitals now? I would really like to get going if I can." I give him a 'please let me go' look. They shouldn't be fawning over me, I should be worrying about them. They are my people to protect. I will let them today though because I am a little afraid. I'm not sure if it was the carbon monoxide that made me blackout or something else but it has rattled me. Most importantly, why the hell am I not healing?

Chapter 7

After a few hours of checking my vitals and more blood tests, I'm finally allowed to go home. It's almost nine pm by the time I walk through my front gate. I'm so lame, it's Friday evening and all I want right now is my bed. I feel like I want to sleep for days. I have already slept a week's worth of sleep in the last day. How much more can I need? Shifting back into the human realm as I walk up the steps to my house I hear a little fairy jingle coming from my garden. That jingle confirms that one, the house is safe and two, they are asleep. Good, hopefully they had no issues while I was gone.

As my front door swings open I hear the last thing I want to hear right now, my phone. I just want my bed! Ergh... Why now? I could just ignore it and let it go to voice mail, that's what it's been doing the whole time I've been gone. I contemplate this for a few seconds before deciding to just answer it. I see Flick's face on my screen and I'm instantly filled with apprehension. Crap! Why is she calling so late? Is it about Duncan? Gathering up my courage I press the green answer button and put the phone to my ear.

"OMG!! You finally answer your phone. Where the hell have you been all day? I've been trying to call you. I need to talk to you." She whimpers through the phone. My heart sinks even more at the sound of her voice, she's crying. Oh no!

"Hey Flick, I'm so sorry I didn't have my phone on me, I've been sick all day. What's going on, are you ok?" I ask cautiously, I have a suspicion this is going to be bad. She is quiet for a little while and I start to think she may have hung up. Then all of a sudden, she half screams, half sobs down the line.

"HE...HE...HE...HE LEFT ME!... DUNCAN LEFT ME!" I move the phone away from my ear so she doesn't burst my eardrum. Wow, that was loud.

"Oh no Flick I'm so sorry, what happened?" I feel horrible. I knew this was coming, from the moment Willow told me that Duncan and I would now be drawn to each other. Duncan won't be able to be with someone else if his heart belongs to me. Flick is hurting because of me. The one guy my best friend has been crushing on and he turns out to be my soulmate. I know I have no control over fate but I feel like such a terrible friend.

Sobbing she replies "I don't know... I don't know what happened, he sent me a text telling me to meet him at the front gate this morning. I did and he walked right up to me and said it was over. No hello or anything, just said 'We can't continue this, I can't be with you, I'm sorry'. That's it! Something happened, it had to of, we were fine yesterday and... and... and well you saw him. Didn't he seem fine to you?" She doesn't pause for me to respond. I don't think she has even taken a breath. "Before he left he said he was sorry again and that he had no idea how to explain what happened, all he knows is that he couldn't be with me. That doesn't even make sense! To rub salt in the wound, throughout the day he avoided me every time we were in the same vicinity, he acted as if I didn't exist at all. Who the hell does he think he is dumping me like that? Right before work and making me feel like shit! What, he couldn't wait till after work? He had to do it in front of all of his friends and make a mockery out of me.

I wish I never got involved with him. I had a blotchy face all day because every time I thought about him it made me cry." She stops for a minute to finally catch her breath and her tears get worse. Through her shaky breath and tears I hear her say, "Kyra I loved him, I know it was quick and you may think I'm silly as we hadn't known each other that long but I did. I truly loved him and this hurts so much." Flick really starts to cry now. I can hear her shortness of breath coming through the phone, it's as if she is on the verge of hyperventilating.

Crap! What am I going to do? I don't want to lie to her but I can't just come out and say, 'Hey Flick, he left you because of me, he didn't have a choice we are soulmates.' Like come on, I'm not that heartless.

"I'm sorry Flick, I know how much you liked him. How he broke it off is not the right way to go about it but you'll bounce back from this, you always do. You're a beautiful, strong, independent woman. You conquer anything and everything you set your mind too. This is just another bump in the road to finding your real Mr Right. I know you had strong feelings for him and maybe he felt the same way but something mustn't have felt totally right for him. You may never know the why of it but you will get past this, you always do. Do you remember what you said to me last time after Josh broke up with you?"

Josh was another construction worker that Flick dated. They dated for six months before he called it quits and started dating Montana, the news reporter who worked in the neighbouring building. Their relationship however, began long before Flick and Josh were separated and once Flick found out she was crushed. Honestly, I think she was better off. I had a feeling that he wasn't being honest right from the start, turns out I was right.

Flick begins to breath more evenly. It sounds as if she is considering what I just said and is trying to remember what she told me last time this happened. After a few moments she says, "Never love somebody who treats you like you're ordinary.' That's what I said when Josh left. I meant it then but I feel as though it means nothing now, I'm starting to think I'm just ordinary or very boring. There is nothing special about me because if there was, why the fuck do these guys keep leaving me?" She sobs a little and again I feel horrible. If I hadn't met Duncan all of this wouldn't be happening. I would be in bed and Flick would probably be out on a date with him. Instead I am trying to console her while at the same time wishing Duncan was here with his big warm arms around me, kissing my neck and running his big strong hands all over my body. Shaking my head to dislodge the images in my brain, I drop the thought. Get a grip Kyra, you need to stay away from him. You can't let yourself get distracted like this.

"Flick, these guys you've dated don't see how special you really are because they are the ones who are ordinary. They are not 'the one.' Your Mr Extraordinary is still out there and when he does find you, he will treat you like a queen and will shower you with all the love and affection that you deserve. Guys like Josh and Duncan, they don't deserve you. You are way too good for them and I bet they know it too. You are amazing, don't let anyone ever tell you otherwise.

Come on honey, look at you! You look like a damn supermodel, even on your bad days. Why would you just settle for anyone when Mr Right is out there. Don't give up on yourself babe just because of a few losers." Hopefully what I said will cheer her up. I start to smile, she loves it when I talk her up. It boosts her self-confidence and who doesn't need a little lift from time to time. Flick definitely does at the moment. She is amazing and there is absolutely nothing wrong with her but she never sees it.

"You know what Kyra you're right, they don't deserve me, I deserve better. I am strong... I am powerful... I am independent... and I can get through this. It's like you said, I am unstoppable when I want something. I do want extraordinary, not ordinary. Even though I feel like a complete idiot for just saying all that to you." She giggles for a moment, "I do feel better though. Thanks Kyra, you always know what to say to make me feel good about myself. You're amazing! Sorry for calling you up so late, I've been trying to get a hold of you all day. Connor said you are sick, are you ok?" We continued chatting for a while and by the time we ended our call she sounded so much better. I still feel horrible that I can't explain what really happened with Duncan but it's better her not knowing. If she was to ever find out the truth it would be a mess, I would lose my best friend all for some guy. A guy I never wanted in the first place.

After we've hung up I feel as if I could just drop to the floor, I'm so tired. Looking up at the clock on the wall, my eyes fly wide open. Are you kidding me? Its eleven pm already! I was on the phone for two hours, no wonder I'm so tired. Walking into the living room, I decide to lie down on the couch. I would love to go to bed upstairs but right now I'm way too sore to even think about climbing those stairs. Curling up with a fluffy decorative pillow, I reach for my knitted blanket that Elder Willow made me for my three hundredth birthday. Willow said the design is to represent our two realms intertwining, two realms coming together in a giant galaxy swirl. The purple colours within the blanket represent Zagoria and the blue resembles the Earth's atmosphere, all the things I strive to protect, my world and theirs. It's beautiful!

Lying on my left side I face the inside of the couch as my right arm throbs too much to even think about lying on my back. This is going to be fun. I'm a restless sleeper, I never sleep in the same position let alone for an entire night. Curling up a little more I try to get as comfortable as I can as I close my eyes. I pray that sleep comes easy for me tonight, I don't remember ever being this tired. I haven't used the power of the sun for a very long time though and forgotten how much it drains me. I feel my body starting to relax as slumber begins to take hold. Many things cross my mind as I start to drift off but there is one that continually comes to the front of my consciousness, the one person I can't stop thinking about...Duncan.

Chapter 8

The floor vibrates from the heavy base as people press their bodies up against mine. Party smoke fills my lungs. People are laughing, screaming and singing along to the music that is being played over the speaker, it's exhilarating to be in a place like this. My arms and hips are moving to the beat and I don't recall a time where I ever felt this free, this alive. When have I ever just danced because I wanted to dance and not because it was an obligation of position? The music really starts to pick up and I move my hips faster to keep time with the beat. I want to feel like this forever.

Without warning someone grabs me from behind, pulling my hips flush against theirs. A shocked smile crosses my lips before I start rocking my hips to keep time with theirs. His cologne smells divine, the kind of smell that wraps around you and makes you feel safe. His hold on my hips tightens as he pulls me even closer against him. Rubbing my ass against the front of his jeans I feel his excitement, it starts doing wondrous things to my insides that I've never felt before. Pressing as close to him as I can with my ass, I move my hips faster, needing to feel more. I hear him groan behind me as he removes one of his hands from my hips to sweep away the hair at my neck. Resting my back against him, he leans down kissing the soft spot behind my ear. Oh Wow! My legs begin to feel shaky as he continues his luscious assault. Wrapping his arm around my waist, he holds me even closer as he continues. I lean my head slightly to the left, giving him better access and seeing my invitation, he begins kissing his way down the side of my neck towards my shoulder.

I feel this overwhelming sensation growing in the pit of my stomach as my breathing escalates. Oh my! Don't stop. My heart is beating erratically as he continues nibbling, licking and sucking my neck. I feel like I'm about to explode. Shaking badly, I grab ahold of his arm that is still around my waist for support and as I do this he takes my ear lobe into his mouth and sucks it hard. The sensation is like nothing I have ever felt before and I detonate, crying out as pleasure takes over my entire being. It feels like lightning moving throughout my veins as colours start flashing behind my eyelids like fireworks. Lucky for me the music is so loud that no one notices what has just happened. Breathing hard, I feel my body slowly starting to go slack as it returns to normal.

"Good girl," A smooth voice whispers into my ear before kissing me on the cheek. "You did it baby, you had your very first orgasm," He declares as he turns me around to face him. Duncan... My Duncan, my soulmate... He smiles down at me, threading his fingers into my hair before moving his face closer to mine and I move my face up to meet his. The moment our lips touch is like fire and ice all intertwined, my body repeatedly switches between being hot and cold. I shift my body flush against his as I wrap my arms around his neck, moving my hands into his hair. I pull him closer to deepen the kiss and his lips move with a need that I know all too well. It is the same desire that has been burning within me from the day we met, this desire is scorching and I need him to extinguish this blaze that is burning deep within me.

Breaking the kiss for only a second I move his head to the side so I can whisper into his ear, "I want you." Knowing full well that those three words will cause some sort of reaction. I make eye contact with him and witness passion igniting deep in his cyan blue eyes. Before I can say more, he grabs my face between his two big hands and pulls my lips towards his again. This time when our lips connect, the kiss is harder, more desperate. With a skilful flick of his tongue, he parts my lips. His kiss is salty and sweet, mixed with a hint of beer, it's sexy as hell.

Moving one hand to the small of my back, he pulls me closer as he continues his sweet assault on my mouth. I moan softly as his hand starts moving south towards my ass. Reaching his desired target, he grabs hard while pushing my lower abdomen against his hard cock, his need for me is growing stronger by the second. He wants this and I want to give it to him.

Forgetting where we are, I begin pulling at his shirt, wanting more as my legs begin to shake. "Oh no you don't. The next time you come it's going to be all over me and unfortunately for you we can't do that in here." He denies me as he gazes at all the people surrounding us. Swinging his head from side to side his eyes lock onto to something in the distance, a smile quickly forms on his face before he peers down at me. "Do you want to get out of here?" He inquires. Believing that nothing logical would come out of my mouth right now, I nod. Giving me a broad smile before stepping away from me, he extends his arm and I take it eagerly. I let him lead us towards the exit. There are so many people here that it's like a war zone trying to make our way through. People are dancing and drinking, pumping their fists into the air like their lives depend on it, others spilling their drinks all over the floor as their bodies sway to the music.

After a couple of minutes of fighting the masses, we finally make it outside. The street is surprisingly quiet compared to inside the club and other than the two bouncers, there seems to be no one around. But none of that matters as the person I want is still holding onto my hand. Duncan looks around for a few moments as if he is trying to remember something and without a word, he begins pulling me towards an alleyway off to the side of the club. It's long and dark and kind of scary, it's the kind of passageway that the underworld creatures lurk in. Sensing my anxiety Duncan stops and pulls me into his arms. "Everything will be ok baby, nothing will get to you, not while I'm here," he breathes into my hair after placing a chaste kiss on my forehead. He steps back and continues to lead us deeper into the laneway.

Roughly fifty metres from the entrance a car starts to take shape within the darkness. What is that doing back here? Duncan stops in front of the car and turns around to face me, a wicked grin is plastered on his face. I wonder what he's up to? Taking both my hands in his big ones, he pulls me closer to him as he moves us to lean against it. Going off my very little knowledge of cars this one seems to be expensive; I think it may be a Maserati but I can't be certain. Quickly I try to move away, I don't want to dent it or even leave a fingerprint on it for that matter. Duncan notices my distress and explains.

"It's ok baby, the car's mine." He chuckles under his breath as he tries to pull me back against him. He has this fiery look in his eye and I have a suspicion that he wants to do something on this vehicle that will make a fingerprint on the beautiful paint job look inconsequential.

"Oh, well I don't want to scratch your car. It looks really expensive." I say as I pull my hands out of his and back up a few steps, putting some distance between us. Duncan gives me a hungry look and I wonder if I may have ruined his plan.

"Come on Kyra, you won't scratch it and if you do, I don't give a shit. I want to take you right here, right now," He states as he points at the ground before him "Now get your sexy ass back over here... Don't make me come and get you." He says this in a super sexy alpha tone that leaves no room for argument. I must hesitate a moment too long and before it registers in my muddled brain, he moves away from his car and approaches me with a wicked grin plastered on his face. I'm in trouble now. I know what he wants and I'm not one hundred percent certain I have the strength to say no, all of this is such a turn on. I have never felt this aroused in all my life but am I going to allow him to take me here?

Half heartedly I warn, "Oh no you don't, you stay away from me. I'm not going anywhere near you or that car, I'm staying right here." I back up even further towards the alley wall as he ignores me completely and prowls towards me, there is nothing I can do to stop him. My back hits the wall at the same moment he reaches me, I feel so small standing under this huge man. And that's no easy task. I'm five foot eleven! Placing his hands on either side of my face, he looks down into my eyes as I lift my hands, resting them against his chest. I can feel his heart beating erratically while his chest moves up and down with every breath he takes, the scent of him invading my senses and I just want to bathe in it forever.

He pushes his body against mine and I can feel his growth pressing into my lower abdomen. "You are mine Kyra, always and forever. We are soulmates and I am drawn to you like a moth is to a flame. I will always cherish you, look after you and take care of all your needs, and right now I think you want to be on the hood of my car just as much as I want you there... naked." He whispers the last word into my ear, causing shivers to run down my spine and begins moving his hips in a grinding motion against me. It's becoming increasingly hard to think, he is being so brazen. Staring deep into his eyes I contemplate saying no but disregard that thought almost instantly, he knows exactly what I want because our souls are connected. He can feel me and I am more than ready to give in to him.

Sensing my surrender he lowers his face to mine and electricity ignites from our joined lips, sending shock waves through my veins down to my core. Removing my hands from his chest, I wrap them around his neck and grip his hair tightly, pulling him closer to me. Duncan shifts his position and pushes me up hard against the wall as he moves his hands, sliding them down my body until he stops at my ass.

In one swift movement he grips my ass hard, lifting me and I automatically wrap my legs around his waist. Pressing myself into him, I continue to kiss him at a desperate pace. Abruptly he turns us around and walks back towards his car, stopping at the front of the vehicle. I can tell he wants to put me down but I won't let him, I need to hold onto him for a little bit longer. I have suddenly become all too aware of where this is heading and my heart is now pounding from nerves rather than excitement. He knows I am a virgin and as if he can sense my anxiety, he breaks our kiss and rests his forehead against mine for a few moments. I think he's trying to calm himself down before he attempts to reassure me.

"It's okay baby, I understand this is all new for you. It does crazy things to me to know that I'll be your first and I promise with all my heart that I would never do anything to hurt you... It might sting a little at first but we will take it slow... You're so strong and beautiful, just let me show you how great we can be together," he whispers to me as he stares into my eyes. I really want to say yes and I don't know why I haven't yet, it's not like I'm scared or anything and I know I'm more than ready. *Duncan will take care of me, so what's stopping me?*

I'm aware that it will hurt, I've read books about what it feels like to lose your virginity and I'm not afraid. *Like come on, I'm 347 years old and still a virgin! I'm seriously the oldest virgin alive. This sexy man wants me, so why am I stopping him?* Gazing into his eyes I feel his need burning into me. I process these questions for a few more seconds then surrender to my desire. I'm going to do it; I'm going to give him what we both desperately want.

Placing both my hands on either side of his face I lean back a little, longing and need is plastered all over his face. He looks up at me from underneath his beautiful, long lashes and my yearning intensifies. Taking a deep breath, I say the one word that will seal both our fates, "Okay." Duncan gifts me with an overwhelming pantie dropping grin and pulls me forward, claiming my mouth once more. He moves his hands, slowly, sliding me down his body until my butt hits the side of the bonnet. Leaning forward he gives me one last kiss before shifting to push me back against the car.

For a few moments he just stares at me all sprawled out on the bonnet. My blonde hair is everywhere, my lips have become full and plump from all the kissing and my cute little black dress is hiked up around my waist exposing my silky, black G-string underneath. My legs are still wrapped around his waist and a sexy grin appears on his face as he raises his hands to unbutton his blue shirt.

"You look so beautiful like this Kyra, I look forward to the day where I can see you fully naked but today, this will have to do." *Mmmm... I look forward to seeing you naked too.* As slow as a snail he undoes each button in turn, biting his lips as his eyes continue to rake over me. His fingers graze the inside of my thigh as he moves to the last button and I gasp loudly as the touch sends shockwaves up my leg. He chuckles from my reaction and I have to bite down on my bottom lip hard to force myself to keep quiet. After what feels like hours, he finally pulls the two sides of his shirt apart and slides the garment to the ground, exposing his god-like abs. *Whoa! This man is fit. I can see every line, every curve of every muscle. Yummm...*

"If you keep looking at me like that baby, I'll have to put the shirt back on. I don't want to distract you from the best part of me now, do I?" He smirks as he grips his hardness through his jeans. *Mmm, he is such a tease. His confidence is such a turn on.* Needing more sensation I slowly rock my hips up and down, feeling him rubbing up against me and sigh as the pleasure begins to build. He grabs my hips and pins me down against the bonnet, preventing me from moving. I let out a frustrated cry and say, "Hey! That's not fair."

"Patience baby, you need to relax, you will get what you want soon enough... Trust me, there is nothing I want more than to fuck you right now. But this is your first time so I'm going to make it last a little longer for you." His words are smooth and precise as he moves his hand, raking it over my breast, my stomach, stopping just above my abdomen.

"What you're doing to me is torturous." I'm kind of giggling and sobbing as the last word leaves my mouth. *This is so not fair, why does he get to decide when things are going to happen?*

"Come on Kyra, I'm just trying to have a little fun and savour you."

"I'm not finding it funny," I grumble.

Removing his hand from my abdomen, he starts running his finger down the centre of my panties. "Is this what you want?" He asks huskily as he ever so slowly runs his finger up and down, teasing and tickling the sweet spot between my legs. "Oh I think it is, I can feel how wet you are." The sensation is exhilarating, I never knew something could feel this good. Pushing with my hips, I thrust up to meet his finger as he brings it back down against me. "You're ready for me, aren't you?"

"Mmhmm," seems to be the only response I can muster. I don't think I could conjure up a single word even if I tried at this point. My hips begin to rock faster as I try to get closer to his finger, the sensation deep inside me continues to build and I think I'm going to explode. I need to feel him, need him to press harder. My breathing becomes heavy as my back lifts off the car. *I'm so close, I feel it, I'm almost there.* A sudden chill hits the apex of my thighs as Duncan removes his hand and I slump back down onto the car.

"Why did you stop?" Asking more angrily than I had intended.

"As I told you before, the next time you to come, it's going to be on me. So quit pouting." *Pouting, who the hell does he think he is? He can't just bring me to the brink of climax and then stop. That's bullshit! Why is he making me wait so long?* My temperature rises the more I think about it. I need to calm down, there is no point overreacting. *He said he would look after me and I trust him but it is just so maddening.*

"Are you ready baby?" He asks, breaking into my thoughts *Did I miss something?* Looking back up at Duncan all my inner turmoil melts away, he is gazing at me with so much love and devotion. *How can I ever stay mad at him?* I rake my eyes over his body to appreciate this beautiful man in front of me and it's only then that I now realise he has removed his pants and is palming his hard length. *OH...MY...GOSH! This is happening, it's actually happening.*

My nerves kick back into overdrive and I begin to shake a little. Swallowing past the hard lump that has formed in my throat, I nod my head eagerly. Chuckling a little, he moves my G-string to the side and slides his finger into my wet folds.

"Mmm... You're so ready for me baby. This might sting, so hold onto me.... Ok?" I offer him a nervous smile and nod. He moves his body over mine and adjusts himself so he is in line with my entrance, positioning his arm above my head which brings his face closer to mine. "I love you," he whispers into my ear before pressing his lips against mine. At the same moment he thrusts deep inside me and stills. *Oh...* My eyes fly open from the shock of the pain. It is excruciating and I grip him tightly, pulling his body close to mine. *Wow, that hurts! I knew it was going to be painful, I just didn't expect it to be anything like this.*

"Shit!... Baby, are you ok?" His breathing is heavy as he pulls his face away from mine to look into my eyes. An uncontrollable tear rolls down the side of my face and the concern in his eyes almost makes me cry. "I'm ok, I just didn't expect it to be anything like that. I'm alright, I just need a moment to adjust." I give him a reassuring smile. *Hopefully, that will ease some of his concern.*

"Okay," he breathes as he leans back slightly. Without adjusting himself inside me, he moves to the side and kisses me next to my left eye, exactly where the tear fell only moments ago. I think he is feeling a little guilty for hurting me, he must have felt my pain through our connection the moment he pushed through my inner wall. Giving me another kiss, on the cheek this time, he moves to lay his head upon my chest and gives me a comforting hug. *What a cutie...*

A minute or so later, the burning has disappeared and I'm ready for Duncan to move again. "OK, I'm ready now." He raises his head from my chest and peering down at me, gives me an assessing smile. Seeing the confirmation he was searching for within my eyes, he positions his arm above my head again and my heart flutters as he begins to move. The sensation is incredible as he slowly rocks his hips back and forth, trying to be as gentle as he can. In this moment it's just us. The world doesn't exist; there is no war, no light versus dark, just Kyra and Duncan. I love him with all my heart and trust that he will never hurt me, he is my saviour and I am his. *However right now though, I need him to move, I need him to make love to me with all that he is.*

"Faster," is the only word I breathe while clinging to him, the sensations building up again. With this invitation, he picks up the pace and starts to pound into me. My moans could wake the neighbourhood but I really don't care, I've never felt this alive in my entire life. He makes me feel like I'm flying and I never want to come back down. My body starts to shake and I know that I'm close. Duncan must feel it too because he thrusts even faster. My arms are holding him tightly around his neck and I lift my legs to wrap them around his back, allowing him to thrust deeper. This new position is incredible and my head falls to lie on the bonnet of the car. I have never felt anything like it and I think I'm about to combust.

"Come for me baby, let me feel you come all over my cock." He whispers into my ear. His softly spoken words are the accelerant to my flame and I moan louder as my body shakes violently, my release.

Chapter 9

Jolting awake, I'm delirious for a few seconds. I blink back the fogginess that lines my vision, a lingering tingly feeling washes through my body. *Where am I?* Lifting my head I see that I'm still on the couch, exactly in the same position where I fell asleep. I don't think I moved at all, that's a new one for me. Still feeling like death, I distractedly shift my right arm but am stopped as an agonising pain shoots down towards my fingers. *What the... Sleep should have healed me but by the feel of it, it's only getting worse. What is going on?* Trying not to panic I sit up and awkwardly rub my face with my left hand. Gazing around my living room, I sigh as I realise that I am completely alone.

"Was that seriously just a dream?"

I'm not only thinking about Duncan during the day now, but dreaming about him too, can this get any worse? I move to get up from the couch but have to sit back down as dizziness overcomes me. *What in the world is happening to me? I never get sick and I always heal, something is wrong.* Looking back down at my arm I see black blood seeping through the bandage. I need to go see the nurses today. Hopefully they have figured out what is happening to me. Moving slowly I get up onto shaky legs and once I feel like I have gained some balance, I gradually make my way to the kitchen. Passing the window I notice the sun is setting over the hills behind my house. *What? That can't be right.*

Looking up at the clock, I see that it's seven-thirty in the evening. "Are you kidding me? I've been asleep the whole day!" *I'm not healing, I feel like crap which never happens and now I'm sleeping well over 12 hours straight.* I'm freaking out, I need to see a nurse as soon as possible, however with the way I'm feeling right now I don't think I'll be able to go anywhere. *How will I get word to them? Phones don't work in Zagoria.* Picking my brain I come up with an idea. *Might not be a bad idea to get Willow involved too.*

Stumbling through my back door I walk into my garden and shift into my realm. My bones are aching from so much movement but I push forward, needing help and it's essential that I get it immediately. I don't know how much more I'll be able to handle. Mustering all my strength, I have to stop myself from screaming as I move my arms around in a wide circle and conjure up a wisp. They are beautiful little mermaid beings that are green in colour but transparent to the eye, that hover above the ground. They are quiet creatures that do not speak but they communicate through musical sounds that only us Zagorian's can hear and understand. They are nimble and quick and can fly which makes them very efficient and just so happens to be what I need right now. Having lost most of my energy due to conjuring the wisp, I sit at a nearby table and the wisp follows. This is not a good sign, I am weak and defenceless.

Luckily I am at home, my home right now is the safest place for me. I may not be able to protect myself, but my girls can.

"Good evening my dear friend, I'm in dire need of your services. Could you please seek out nurse Lexi? She is currently at the Army of the Light compound. Tell her that Princess Kyra is not doing too well and that her presence is requested immediately at the Princess's home. Once you have finished there, please then seek out Elder Willow at her home and request her attendance here as well." The tiny wisp gave a swift nod in acknowledgement. "Thank you for your assistance friend. Journey on with haste please." And as quick as the wind, the wisp is gone.

I'm sitting in place for what feels like seconds before a hand taps me on the shoulder, startling me. "Sorry Your Highness, I didn't mean to scare you." Lifting my head, I have to squint at nurse Lexi as I'm finding it hard to focus. *I have a ripper of a headache.* "Are you alright? I received your wisp and came right away." Before I can respond, she takes a good look at me and inhales sharply; I must look worse than I feel. "Oh my, Your Highness, we must get you inside immediately so I can assess you properly. You do not look well at all. Have you contacted an Elder?... Here let me help you up." She doesn't give me a chance to respond and starts helping me to stand.

I'm grateful that Lexi is here because if she wasn't, I don't think I'd be able to stand up on my own. I feel so weak and drained, something is happening to me that I cannot explain. Fear and dread sit like rocks in the pit of my stomach. If Lexi can't figure out what is happening, I think I may be in trouble.

"Thank you Lexi, I don't know what I'd do without you right now... And yes, I have sent word for Elder Willow. She needs to know what's going on here, I believe she will be here shortly," I finally manage to respond, speaking through laboured breathes as we make our way up the back steps and into my house. We enter the living room and with help I manage to make it to the couch I was sleeping on not too long ago. *Man I need to sit down. I'm so drained.* As soon as my butt hits the cushion my front door swings wide open, banging hard against the wall as Willow rushes in. "KYRA! KYRA, WHERE ARE YOU?" She yells from the foyer. Weakly I call out to her, "I'm in here." My words sound far away even to my ears, my breathing has become heavy and I feel as if I could pass out. *The Cerberus bite has to be causing all this, but why? This isn't the first time I have been attacked. Though, I was never bitten by a Cerberus before, maybe my body is just reacting differently to the bite than others. Hopefully this is just a seriously bad side effect that takes longer to heal.*

Willow rushes to where I'm sitting, completely forgetting formalities and begins checking me over. Starting with her hand on my forehead, she checks for a fever, then moves to my eyes to see how they react to bright lights and so on. Willow is doing all the things that Lexi has yet to do but Lexi doesn't stop her. Elders have the authority to do whatever they like, unless I say otherwise, which I don't.

"Kyra darling, you are running a high fever, have you taken anything to bring it down?" She is regarding me as if I'm a small child again. It brings a smile to my lips.

"No I haven't. I've been asleep all day and when I awoke, I called forth the wisp to send for help. I barely had enough energy to walk out the back door let alone the stairs. I'm scared Willow, what is happening to me?" I sob as I put my head in my hands. The movement causes tremendous pain to shoot through my injured arm, making me yelp.

"It's ok sweetie, where is your medicine cupboard? I'll go get you something to calm your fever." Even though I have never needed medication, I have always made sure I had it in the house just in case someone came over requiring it. It made me feel a little bit normal to have the stuff lying around my house and Willow knows that too. Between my tears I tell Willow where to find it and she rushes off up the stairs and out of view, leaving Lexi and me alone.

"Your Highness, may I please check your wound? It looks as if it may need to be redressed." Nodding, I keep my head in my left hand, moving my right arm so Lexi can access it and shrieking as her cold fingers make contact with my overly warm skin.

"Sorry... Tell me if I hurt you ok?"

"Okay," I whisper in response as I feel her untying the bandage from my arm. After a few careful touches and movements, I feel fresh air hit my skin. Lifting my head I take a good look at my arm and shock takes over my entire body. The wound which is full of stitches looks disgusting, reddish-black ooze seeps from the bite and the stitches are turning an off green-purple colour. The stench wafting from the wound is so foul, it reminds me of a rotting corpse, it smells of death. Glancing up at Lexi, she too is staring at my arm, she hasn't moved an inch since she removed the dressing and her perplexed expression doesn't do much to calm my wayward nerves.

"What is it Lexi? Why am I not healing, is it because of the bite?" I ask her on a shaky breath.

"Honestly Your Highness I have no clue why you're not healing. All the other soldiers who were bitten are healing just fine but for some reason, you are not. This isn't good and I'm sorry that I have no further answers for you. All I can do right now is clean it up and dress it as best as I can. We will keep a close eye on it and hopefully your natural healing will kick in soon and you will be right as rain in no time." Before I have a chance to respond, Willow comes barrelling down the stairs. "I found them..." She announces this as she raises a packet of pills in her hand, bypassing the lounge room and heading straight for the kitchen. Within a flash Willow emerges with a glass of water in her hand.

"Here missy take these." Taking my left arm she places the pills into my hand, watching me as I put them in my mouth, before handing me the glass of water. Taking a big gulp and swallowing both the pills in one go, I sigh as the water slides down, it feels heavenly on my parched throat. *I didn't realise I was so thirsty until now.* Finishing off the glass, I place it on the coffee table before returning to a comfortable position.

"Good girl, now let me have a look at that arm of yours." Lexi quickly moves out of the way to make room for Willow. I give her a sympathetic smile to let her know that I completely understand just how bossy Willow can be and that we both just need to roll with it. She returns my smile before curtsying quickly and walking out of the room, leaving Willow and me alone.

"Hmm... Well sweetie I'm going to be honest with you, this really doesn't look good. I think we're going to have to chop it off."

"WHAT!" Whipping my head in her direction I stare at her in disbelief. *She can't be serious!*

"Gotcha!" She cackles to herself. *That really wasn't funny at all. I can't believe she did that.*

"Come on Willow this isn't funny, something is seriously wrong here and you're making jokes. I am seriously freaked out here. How would you like it if someone was making jokes about you and you were in my current state?" Slouching back in my seat as a wave of dizziness takes over. *I mustn't get emotional, I need to remain calm.* There is only so much I can handle right now. I feel weak, drained even and there is nothing left within me but the constant pull towards the man I cannot have. The link that binds us together is calling for him, I can feel it. If I wanted to and had enough energy, I bet I could walk out my front door and follow that link and it would lead me straight to him, but right now all I can do is sit here and wait. *Wait for what exactly? I don't really understand this feeling but I feel as if I am waiting for something.*

"I'm sorry sweetie I didn't mean to upset you, I'm just trying to add a little light to this terrible situation. I conversed with the other elders earlier at the hanger about your injuries and they too have never seen anything like this before. We are not sure what is happening but all we can do right now is watch over you and wait it out. Hopefully, whatever it is will fix itself up sooner rather than later."

"What if it doesn't? What if whatever is going on..." Shaking my head I take a deep breath, trying to calm my nerves. "Willow, what if it's killing me, what then?" A few tears slip down my cheeks as I try to hold onto my composure. I've never been this scared about anything in my life, I'm terrified to think about my future, Zagoria's future.

"I will not even think of such an outcome and neither should you. You are so strong Kyra, remain positive. Positive thoughts lead to positive mind and body, ok?"

"I'll try," *Easier said than done.*

For a few minutes we sit there in silence and I focus on my breathing. The pills must be starting to take effect as my aches begin to lesson, my headache is almost non-existent and my fever is disappearing. *Doesn't mean I'm feeling any better though.*

Willow sits there staring at me with a confused expression on her face, that's not a good look when it's coming from an elder. It's a bit concerning, they're usually never confused about anything. They are known for their wealth of knowledge and guidance, so if the elders don't know, it has to be bad. Overwhelmed by this thought I close my eyes and I will myself not to think. I'm so tired and before I know it, I'm asleep.

Something warm is pressed against my arm and I'm awoken by the resulting sting. "That really burns you know," I croak out as I try to sit up a little straighter.

"Oh, I'm sorry Your Highness, I didn't mean to wake you. I just thought seeing as you were asleep and your wound still isn't looking any better, I would give it a good thorough clean. This is just a little disinfectant; it should help prevent any infection." She moves the wet cloth over my wound, rubbing in soft slow circles as she speaks. If it wasn't stinging so much, it would actually be quite relaxing.

"Thank you Lexi, I really appreciate it." I tense up as the stinging intensifies, trying not to disclose my discomfort. *Man that stings!*

Oblivious to my internal struggles Lexi replies, "It's my pleasure Your Highness but I need you to relax now, ok? It'll be done in no time and then you can go back to sleep and rest. Promise" She continues rubbing the disinfectant all over my arm and I flinch a few times as I try to remain still. It's difficult as the wound burns with a fiery throb every time Lexi touches it and I am struggling to stay awake as exhaustion tries to pull me under. *The quicker we finish the quicker I can go back to sleep.*

Half an hour later she is done, my arm is clean and all bandaged up, the rancid smell is no longer present. "You did a magnificent job, thanks Lexi, you're a miracle worker," I say appreciatively.

"Thank you Your Highness, but truly it was nothing. Please ensure you don't get the bandage wet, if you want to bathe I would recommend you have a bath so you can keep it out of the water. Now, if you don't need anything else, I best be off."

"Oh, ok, thank you. I'm sorry I kept you up most of the night tending to me but I really appreciate it."

"It's no troubles at all, I'm just sorry I can't be of further help to you. If you do need me again though please don't hesitate to call, I'm always available."

"Thank you Lexi."

"Good night Your Highness" Lexi curtsies, before walking out the back door.

Breaking the silence of the now quiet room, Willow asks, "Are you sure you don't want me to stay here with you?" She is standing at the foot of the couch, staring at me with her hands on her hips. The entire time Lexi was cleaning my arm, Willow was pushing for me to let her stay the night so she could keep an eye on me.

"Yes Willow I'm sure, please go home and rest, I'll call for you if I need further help. Right now all I want to do is sleep and I won't sleep properly if I know that you are staring at me all night. As an old fart, you need your sleep too, so you should go home and get some rest." I smile as I know the old comment will get a rise out of her. She hates it when I call her old, even though we both know she is.

"Who are you calling an old fart? I should wash your mouth out for such accusations young lady!"

"I'm just getting my payback for your comment earlier, saying we should cut my arm off."

"You're lucky I love you girly, or I wouldn't hesitate." I laugh at her response, this banter between us is one I will always treasure. I don't have a fun and carefree relationship with any of the other elders, they are always formal and remind me of my royal title. My relationship with Willow is so much more.

"Come on oldie, give me your best shot. Even in this bad state I bet I could still take you." I giggle as I raise both my fists up in a guard motion, trying to act like the movement didn't affect me at all.

"Don't push your luck. You couldn't take me when you were a youngling and I bet you couldn't take me now either, you're getting on in years too 'Your Highness'." She says while smiling to herself, probably remembering my younger years when she used to whip my butt.

"Hey! I did get you on the ground that one time during training, or have you forgotten that?"

"Ah yes, yes I remember that. You were showing me something that Elder Kit had taught you. That was a great manoeuvre. Do you still use it?"

"All the time."

"Good" She looks to the ground, suddenly appearing to be saddened by something. Before I can ask her what's wrong she snaps out of it and shakes her head, moving towards the head of the couch. "Alright girly, if you don't need anything else, I'm going home. Call me if you need me, ok?"

"I will, good night Willow." She leans forward and gives me a kiss on the forehead, whispering "Goodnight sweetie" before walking off towards the back door and locking it as she leaves. I smile to myself. *I really love that woman.* I get comfy, rearranging myself to avoid causing any more discomfort to my injuries and relax back into the couch, I close my eyes and dream of Duncan.

Chapter 10

Light streams in through the lounge room windows as my eyes flutter open. *Please don't let it be Monday.* Rolling onto my back, I stretch as best I can with my bad arm. The shooting pain I get from moving it tells me I still haven't healed. *What else is new?* I can tell the pain medication wore off while I was sleeping because I feel even worse than I did before. *I didn't think that was even possible.*

Sitting up slowly, I try to gather the strength to stand up. Any quick movement will make me dizzy, so I know I should proceed with caution. *Maybe I should have let Willow stay here, just so she could help me go to the bathroom. This really sucks.* With wobbly legs I get up into a standing position. My legs tremble with every step I take as I stumble my way out of the room, around the corner and finally reach my destination. *It's a miracle I didn't fall over.*

After finishing in the bathroom, I make my way down the hall and into the kitchen. Stumbling over to the bench, I grab my phone and with shaky fingers I press the unlock button and my screen comes to life. "Oh thank Zagoria... it's still Sunday." I breathe out a sigh of relief. *It may be noon Sunday, but it's still Sunday. I have until eight am tomorrow morning to figure out what the hell I'm going to do. Especially if I haven't healed by then.*

My stomach rumbles, reminding me that I haven't eaten anything since I left for Zagoria on Friday afternoon. *No wonder I feel so weak.* Hobbling over to the refrigerator I peer inside, looking for anything edible. Usually, I go shopping on a Saturday to restock my fridge but as I open the door, it looks as if someone already went and did it for me. Looking over the contents I notice there is a sticky note attached to a container full of salad on the middle shelf. Taking the note from the container I read, 'Eat up sweetie, this contains all the yummy goodness your body needs.' *Of course she got me food, gosh that woman is my hero.* Grabbing the container and a fork out of the draw, I carefully sit down at the table and devour my food until there is nothing left.

Eating something should have made me feel better but it hasn't, it has made me feel worse. *I feel like I'm going to be sick.* Nausea rolls deep within my stomach and my mind instantly has thoughts of one of the Dark Princes minions, however the sensation isn't quite right. Darting quickly out of the kitchen I head directly to the bathroom. I barely make it to the toilet as all my lunch comes rifling back up. *This is just perfect.* After the heaving subsides I take stock of myself and feel it's ok to get up off the floor. I move to the sink and splash cold water on my face, it feels amazing on my clammy skin. I wipe my face with the hand towel hanging on the wall and it's then that I finally get a glimpse of myself.

My fire is dim and deflated, my green eyes are bloodshot even though I've had plenty of sleep, my skin is grey instead of its normal golden hues, I look as if I'm dying. My cheeks and eyelids have sunken in and my lips have lost their fullness. *I'm like a damn skeleton. How am I going to explain my appearance at work tomorrow? I should get Willow to call Connor again in the morning and tell him I won't be in. I will scare the pants off all my colleagues if I go in looking like this.*

Tearing my eyes away from the mirror I shake my head as I make my way back into the living room. I'm about to lie down on the couch when I realise my blanket is not there. *Where is it?* Looking around I see it draped over the back of my reading chair in the far corner. Willow or Lexi must have put it there earlier. Walking over to retrieve it, nausea and dizziness suddenly attack my body and I don't have time to react as I fall to the ground, smashing my head on something as I go down.

Lying on the floor of my living room, everything is black and pixelated, the whole room is spinning and I feel like I'm going to pass out. *I must stay awake.* I'm losing control of my body and it starts to shift between realms without my say so. I would prefer to be on Earth so I focus with everything I have on staying in this realm. After a few moments, I'm able to concentrate enough to keep myself from shifting and I am able to get my bearings on where I am. I have managed to stop while on Earth and am currently lying on my lounge room floor. I try to blink away the blackness and access my rolling stomach. This isn't the same sort of nausea I felt before, this is something else. *No!* A minion is here and there is nothing I can do to stop it. I'm in no state to fight. I can't even push myself into a sitting position, let alone fight a minion and win.

I'm in serious trouble... And what if it's a hound? My girls won't stand a chance against a hound... It can't break through the barrier but what if it can. What if it does and it hurts them or worse, kills them? The nauseous feeling in my stomach intensifies at the thought and I start to panic. *What if it gets in here, what am I going to do?... I can't defend myself; I can't even get up off the floor.* I attempt to push myself up, but I can't move my arms or fingers. *Why can't I move?... Am I paralyzed?... OH MY GOD, I can't move!*

Panicking now as I try with all my might to get up but nothing happens. The only thing I can move is my eyes and even my vision is starting to get blurry as tears begin to roll down my face. *I'm going to die. I'm going to die alone and defenceless in my home, I won't be going out in a blaze of glory like I always hoped.* The overpowering feeling of hopelessness that suddenly overcomes me knocks the breath from my lungs and I find myself silently begging for help. *Someone please help me, save me... please?* I'm not ready to die and at the realisation that this is an imminent possibility, the tears really start to fall, I'm so overcome by emotion. The intense sadness I feel from not being able to defend my girls and myself is staggering but the most painful thought of all is knowing that I will never get a chance to experience love with my soulmate. Never get to experience his warm embrace, his rough hand in mine or his lips on my skin. We will never get the chance to make those memories together.

As I begin to comprehend the enormity of lost opportunities the front door swings open wide, hitting the wall with a tremendous BANG! It sounds like a gunshot ricocheting through my entire house, the sound making me flinch. *Silver lining, at least I know my body can still react to noises. The downside, I'm probably about 10 seconds away from my demise.* I can't see the creature properly due to the lingering tears in my eyes, as it stumbles through the walkway, coming straight for me. *This is the end; I've been rendered useless and I'm going to die here on my lounge room floor.* The black figure moves towards me slowly, like it's taking its time to taunt me. *Yeah, let's rub salt into the already festering wound why don't we?*

It's about two metres away from me when it suddenly drops to its hands and knees and begins crawling over to where I'm lying. My eyes must be playing tricks on me or my mind has summoned an amazing life like hallucination, because when the creature finally gets close enough for me to see clearly, it's not a dark minion at all, it's Duncan and all thoughts of a minion leave my mind, my mate has found me. It's as if my thoughts conjured him out of thin air.

Concern is written all over his face and I'm cognizant enough, that I don't miss the fact that he too looks like death. His skin is the same greyish tone as my own, his eyes are bloodshot and have lost their shine and it appears that he has also lost weight. *What the hell!... What is wrong with him and how did he find me?... What is he doing here?*

"Shit Kyra... Fuck, there is so much blood." With a panicked expression on his face, he reaches towards me to check my pulse. Without warning, agonising pain erupts from that single touch and I scream from the onslaught as electricity shoots through my veins. It's as quick as lightning and power surges within me as I suddenly regain my strength. I grab a hold of Duncan's arm, afraid that if we separate this connection whatever is happening will stop. *I need it to continue as it's healing me and I think it's healing him too.* Looking up at him, I watch as his cheeks fill out, the shine in his eyes return and his taw glow restored. Within seconds he appears to be back to his normal self.

"Duncan..." I utter through laboured breaths, the surge of power that is now flowing through my veins has temporarily taken my breath away. "...What are you doing here?... How did you even find me?" He continues to stare at me but doesn't respond. *Ok, this is getting awkward.* I stare at him for a few moments waiting for him to respond to my questions. Realising this is clearly not going to happen, I slowly push myself up into a sitting position. This must be the encouragement he needs because all of a sudden, he jumps back from the movement but continues to stare in the same direction.

It's only now that I am in a sitting position that I notice, he wasn't staring at me at all, he was staring at the ground beside my head. Turning my head to see what he is fixated on, I see all the blood and he wasn't kidding when he said there was a lot. *How in the world am I still alive? The loss of that much blood should have killed me. I can't believe I remained conscious.* The stain on the floor is about four feet in diameter. Tentatively I touch the back of my head, it's all sticky. *Gross! Thankfully, the gash appears to have healed. That's good news, I guess. But how is all of this even possible? I should be dead!*

Through all the confusion, I am still aware enough to remember the incoming minion. I stop and feel for it, but it seems to of disappeared. *Strange.* Duncan still hasn't said a word, so I tentatively raise my hand to his face and stroke his stubbled cheek with my thumb. *He's here, he's really here. I don't know how or why, but I'm so glad he is here.* He lifts his eyes to meet mine and finally says, "I thought I was losing you Kyra... with that much blood around you, I was sure you were going to die." He whispers the last part, as a tear escapes the side of his eye. Moving my hand, I wipe it away with my thumb. Sudden awareness of what I just did, makes me blush. Even though we don't know one another, I feel as if I have known him forever. *I need to remember boundaries.*

"I see why you were so worried; I would have been too if I saw someone lying on the ground like that, in all that blood. It's ok now though, I'm fine, see?" I lift my arms in a grand display, to show him that I am completely unscathed. He just looks at me and I feel like an idiot for my display, I giggle nervously. Duncan offers me a bright smile which makes my embarrassment worth it. After lowering my arms, I belatedly realise that my arm didn't hurt when I moved it, I look at the bandage around my arm and with quick fingers I unravel the binding, revealing the semi-healed tattered mess. Although it no longer hurts, it still looks quite gruesome.

A sharp intake of breath catches my attention and I look up to see Duncan staring at the mess that is my arm. He grabs my bicep, pulling it close to his face, trying to get a better look at the artwork of stitches. "WHAT THE FUCK! What happened?" He growls as he shifts his gaze from my arm to my face in disbelief, his smile has quickly been replaced with anger. *Shit! How am I going to be able to explain this one and why is he so upset? I get it, it doesn't look appealing and all, but... why is he so worked up?* Even if we had known each other longer, I won't be able to explain it properly until I know if he is from Zagoria or not. I'm pretty sure he is but I can't be sure. I need to tread carefully.

"I need you to clarify one thing for me first." This response does not impress him, he is angry as all hell and I don't know if it's because of me or the stitches. I sit patiently and wait for him to respond. Realising I will not explain anything without his compliance, he takes a few deep breaths and manages to calm himself down enough to answer me.

"Fine, what?" he huffs. *Oh, you ain't getting anything outta me with that attitude! Who do you think you are buddy?*

"Calm your tone or I won't tell you."

"Like hell you won't, this is a big fucking cut you have here Kyra. You didn't have it on Thursday when I met you,

I think I would have noticed. So, where the fuck did you get it?" He growls in my face.

"Ok fine! Geez, back off! You said it yourself, we only just met Thursday. I don't really know anything about you. I just need you to answer one quick question before I tell you because it's important." I pause and take a deep breath before I ask him the question that could seal both our fates. "Have you ever heard the word Zagoria?" As the last word leaves my mouth, he gives me a 'do you think I'm stupid look' and I relax. I didn't even notice how tightly wound I was about the possibility of him not knowing my world, until now.

Oblivious to my relief he replies with, "Seriously Kyra? Of course I have, now cut the shit. Where did you get the cut from?"

Sick of the pushy bullshit, I lose my temper. *Who does he think he is to speak to me this way? He may be my soulmate and I get that we have this special connection but seriously dude... Chill!* "Oh, I'm sorry Mr Know-it-all. You know I had to clarify and you know we can't go around telling people of our world and this..." I say pointing to my arm, "...happened in our world. I got bitten by a Cerberus on Thursday night." *If looks could kill, I'm pretty sure I would be dead.*

He jumps to his feet even angrier than before and starts pacing the room. *What is his deal? What has got him so livid?* His breathing has become heavy and he begins pulling at his hair. *I bet if this was a cartoon, he would have smoke coming out of his ears too*. I smile at the thought and get to my feet. I walk over to him and rest my hands on his shoulders, forcing him to look at me. Although he is pissed and I am completely confused by this situation, I feel this intense urge to comfort him.

"It's ok Duncan. We took down the whole nest and although we lost a lot of good men and women out there, if we hadn't taken them down when we did, the damage would have been even greater. Especially if they managed to get out and go hunting as a pack."

"A nest!" He exclaims as he stares down at me dumbfounded. "Are you fucking kidding Kyra? My mate goes hunting down nests and I have no fucking clue that it's even happening. Well that's just peachy isn't it?" He says this more to himself than to me and pulls himself out of my grasp, and begins pacing the room once more.

"Come on Duncan. If you're a Zagorian, you would know who I am and what I must do. It's my job, I have to protect everyone, I have no choice in the matter. Why are you making such a big deal of this anyway? It's not like it's the first time I've taken down a nest. I've been doing this my whole life you know."

"Big deal! Are you seriously asking me what the big deal is?" He is fuming and honestly, it's terrifying. We don't know each other well enough for me to understand and decipher his mannerisms. Stopping right in front of me, he stares me down. "Fucking hell Kyra, we are soulmates. We are bound now and forever, linked for as long as we both shall live. Have you not consulted your elder Willow about this?" Irritation crosses his face.

"I did but she didn't say much except that we were linked and that I have to stay away from you." I fire back as my own irritation and anger begins to rise.

"I was told that too but are you sure she didn't say anything else?" A look of scepticism replaces the irritation and I'm fuming. *Who the hell is he to question me? He barely knows me and is treating me this way, well I've had it.*

"Yes, I'm sure that's all she said. What, don't you believe me? Come on then smart arse, what did you get told by the elders that I didn't, huh?" He ponders my question for a moment and he must come to some sort of realisation because I watch him physically calm himself down. He takes a few deep breaths before opening his mouth to speak.

"I'm sorry Kyra, I'm not trying to upset you, but you have to understand something, the elders obviously told me a lot more about soulmates than just being linked. I'm not sure why Willow didn't tell you. Perhaps she doesn't want you to know the rest, maybe she wanted to keep it a secret from you."

"What on Earth are you talking about?" He steps forward and takes my small hands in his big ones, his hands are rough with age and I tilt my head up to look at him.

"Kyra, the elders told me that if either one of us were to die, the other would die too. That is why it's such a 'big

deal'?... Kyra, if you go into battle and you die, I will die too."
NO WAY! You have got to be kidding me!

"Which Elder told you this? There has to be a mistake, this can't be true." *I don't believe him. I can't believe him. Why would Willow withhold this information from me? This is huge and definitely something I should have been made aware of.*

"There is no mistake, what I have said is true. I knew Elder Snow wasn't lying the moment I came through your front door. I was drawn to you; my body was seeking yours because you were injured, my soul was pushing me to help yours. Don't you see, if you are injured I feel it, if you need me I know. You were calling for me and you didn't even know it.

I contacted Elder Snow yesterday and arranged to see him when I started feeling odd. I was lacking in energy, sleeping long periods of time and honestly, I just felt vile. He said that now our souls are aware of each other, we are now connected in every possible way. He told me all there is to know about soulmates, how we are linked, how we are drawn to each other. We are unable to heal when we are apart and that we can only heal each other by touching. Didn't Willow tell you any of this?" I shake my head in response. There are a million questions rolling around in my head and that is all I am capable of communicating right now. *Why would Willow keep all this from me? I just don't understand.*

"Far out Kyra, she told you absolutely nothing! How could she keep such vital information away from you? For fuck sake, we could have died if I didn't get here when I did. Your body has been calling for me the whole weekend and I didn't realise it until it was almost too late. Elder Snow said I would feel it when you would need me. Take your arm for instance, you said you got bitten on Thursday night, right? Was it around seven-ish?"

"I don't know maybe, why?" I nod as I try to recall all that's happened between now and then.

"I was out drinking at the bar with a few mates from work and around that time I started to feel off, dizzy even. I thought the drinks were hitting me too hard or something, so I went home and tried to sleep it off. I woke up around noon on Friday feeling like shit. My body was in agony, not the normal response I get from drinking the night before. I knew something wasn't quite right, so I went to Zagoria and met with Elder Snow and he told me everything. He told me that if I was feeling this way, there was no doubt you would be too, maybe even worse. He told me I needed to find you as soon as possible. It took me so long to get here because it took me a while to come to terms with it all.

Then this morning, I woke up feeling even worse. I knew I couldn't leave it any longer, I had to find you. I felt the pull and I followed it; I was roughly halfway here when I felt your body screaming for mine. You were terrified and your pain Kyra, I felt everything through the link and it was petrifying. I was so afraid of what might be happening that I used all my remaining energy and sprinted the rest of the way here and when I got through the door and saw all the blood, I thought... Honestly, I thought you were on the brink of death, you weren't moving at all. Then I saw you blink and I have never felt such relief. I knew I had to get to you, to touch you so you would heal, I wasn't about to lose you before I even got a chance to know you.

When we touched, I felt it! We regained our strength and it really hit me then, that I had the power to help you yesterday. I was just too focused on myself and admittedly freaking out a little, to come here and help.... Kyra, please forgive me. I'm so sorry. We could have died today, all because of my selfish act. I've never been so afraid of anything in my life and it wasn't because I would die, it was because you would too and I could not and will not accept that. I am so sorry it took me so long to get here. I've been on my own for so many years and I'm used to just taking care of myself but I have you to look out for now too.

I barely even know you but I care for you more than anything in this world. It would wreak me if anything ever happened to you. You are my soulmate Kyra and my heart belongs to you." Tears are streaming down my face. I didn't know he was in pain this whole time too and it saddens me immensely.

Because information was withheld from me, I unwittingly made him endure my injuries. He cares deeply for me and I believe I feel the same way. My heart belongs to him, now and forever. He is my forever songbird, the love of my life and my light when I pass through the darkness.

"I'm the one who should be sorry Duncan, I didn't know any of that. I spoke with Elder Willow before I even went to that nest and if what you're saying is true, which I believe it is, it means Willow kept this information from me. I'm so sorry I put you through so much pain, I didn't mean to, I just didn't know. Why didn't Willow tell me, why would she withhold such important information from me?" I think on that question for a moment before the answer hits me like a brick. "Oh, Willow..." I sigh her name. "... she didn't tell me because if I had known, I wouldn't have gone on the hunt. I would have neglected my duties to save you from the possibility of any physical harm.

I was created to protect my people but if I had known the truth, that if I was to die, you would die too, I wouldn't have risked it. I would have refused to do what I was created to do, all in the name of love..." I shake my head as another thought occurs to me. "...Though, if she knew that we healed each other, why didn't she say anything? She was here last night and she just let me suffer through it all. How could she have been so heartless?..." My anger flares before another thought pops into my head. "Unless maybe she doesn't know? Perhaps it's information that only some of the elders are privileged to?"

That could be it, she wouldn't have let me deal with all that pain if she knew that just one touch from Duncan could have stopped it all. *I'm sure of it.* Duncan continues to sit there quietly, while I process my thoughts and ramble on. "But why would only some elders have this knowledge and not others? That doesn't make any sense. The elders are supposed to know everything and come on, it's not like they haven't dealt with this sort of thing before, right? They must have if Elder Snow has information on how soulmates work." I contemplate all that Duncan has said. *Maybe Snow is the only one who has dealt with soulmates before. But who were they?* "It is possible that not all of the elders know. Maybe only a few know all the details because they have seen soulmates in action before. Elders like Willow might only know what to look out for but don't know everything else. We need to go see her to clear all this up."

"Are you seriously going to go up to Elder Willow and start demanding answers?" He gives me this sexy smirk as he assesses the determined look on my face and realises that's exactly what I plan to do.

"You're damn right I am, want to come with me? I'm sure she'd be interested to meet you." As he nods his head in agreement to come with me, I point my finger into his chest as my excitement **builds**. *Willow must have a good reason for her actions and I'm sure she would love to meet the man who has stolen my heart, even if she warned me to stay away from him.* If she has never seen soulmates in action before, there is no better day than the present.

Duncan gives me a sour face. "She's not the kind of Elder to ask twenty billion questions, is she?" He crosses his arms and pouts like a little girl, making me laugh.

"Nah, more like a trillion, but you'll be fine. You'll be with me and I'll do most of the talking anyway. You just have to sit there and look handsome. Before we leave though, I really need to have a shower, I stink. Do you mind waiting a few minutes? I won't be long." Winking at him I walk out of the room and head towards the bathroom with the biggest grin on my face. *This should be interesting. I hope we can get some answers but either way, Willow is going to eat him alive.*

Chapter 11

Walking towards the front gate, I realise I need to do something first. "Hey Duncan, can you give me a moment? I just need to go see to something really quick." I must check in with the ladies before I leave and get an update on what they may know about what happened earlier. *I need to make sure they are ok.*

"Yeah sure, take your time. I'll just wait for you out on the street." With that, he walks out the gate and I run over to the small house in my garden.

As I approach I greet them. "Good evening ladies. How are we?" Not prepared for my visit they all scurry around franticly at the sound of my voice, coming to stand in a perfectly straight line in front of me. They curtsy before speaking.

"Good evening Your Highness, we are well. How are you? You are looking much better." They answer me as one, all with big smiles on their faces. It warms my heart to know they care so much about my welfare.

"I'm glad you are all well. I'm doing much better now, all thanks to Duncan. I feel as good as new. However, I need to know, what sort of creature came by earlier? I apologise for not coming out to fight, I was still not strong enough. By the time I was well enough to fight, the creature was gone. Did you have any troubles with it?" Exchanging weird looks, they seem to be debating on how to answer my question. *Am I missing something?*

"We are sorry Your Highness, we never encountered the monster. We felt it coming too however, as soon as it was close enough for us to fight, it ran away. We are unsure as to why, they never turn away from a fight."

"Really! It ran away? I agree, that is strange. No matter, there is no need for an apology ladies. It's not your fault... Anyway, I was just on my way out to go see Elder Willow, I just wanted to check in with you first. I'll be back later. Please keep the house safe for me until I return. See you soon." I wave to them as I walk towards the front gate.

The creature just ran away. Why would something that is sent to kill me just leave? I was in such a weakened state and it's possible they would have known that, it just doesn't make sense. I think this is something else I need to bring up with Willow.

The air outside is cool against my skin, much cooler than I expect for this time of year. Hopefully a cool front is coming, Australia can be very hot in the summer. It's the only downside to living here, the summers are extremely hot and the winters are freezing, although it's not cold enough for it to snow. Flick told me about this place she travels to once a year up in the Australian Alps, she claims they have the "sickest" slopes to go skiing. I've contemplated going with her a few times but I end up changing my mind last minute. I don't have the pleasure of taking a vacation, my job is to find the Prince, not go skiing. No matter how much I wish I could take a break and go on a real holiday. *I wonder what a holiday would be like.*

I realise we have been walking in silence for about two blocks. Well... This is awkward. *Has he really got nothing to say to me? Though, I guess I haven't spoken either. Come on Kyra, this is your chance to get to know the guy. He is your soulmate. Talk to him!*

"So Duncan, what do you like to do for fun?" His response is nothing but silence, I look towards him and realise that he is too busy staring at the sunset to even notice I said anything. *Well that's just great. Now I'm talking to myself. Could this get any more uncomfortable?* We walk a bit further up the road before I attempt to ask him again, this time I make sure he is looking straight forward when I ask.

"I think this would be a great time for us to start getting to know one another, would you agree?" Without a word he just nods his head, continuing to stare forward. *Well that's encouraging... Not.* "Ok... so... What do you like to do for fun? Do you have any hobbies?" This time I know he heard me. A focused expression crosses his face as he thinks about his answer.

"Well, I love to go rock climbing and hiking. There is something about mother nature that captivates me, I love to explore it. Other times I like to go out with my mates on the weekends and go riding, but other than that I don't do much. How about you?" *This is good, this I can work with. Cool and casual conversation. Just what we need, to get to know one another.*

"Hiking, really? Aren't you afraid of the dark minions? Have they ever tried to attack you?" Most of the creatures only attack those who are keepers of the light but I wouldn't put it past them to attack others too." Hikers are perfect for the dark creatures. They usually like to trek in small groups and in quiet locations, which makes them easy targets.

"They show their faces now and then but usually they just leave me alone. I'm not special like you are." He gives me this huge grin as he responds, as if he is proud of himself because the creatures leave him alone. However, the look fades quickly and a look of realisation crosses his face. "Wait! They will be coming after me now won't they? We are linked, so if they kill me, they will kill you too...shit, that sucks! There go my quiet weekends" His demeanour and the look of dismay on his face are quite comical but then I'm sobered by the thought that he is right. His life will change because of our connection. Now we both need to be really careful and that includes factoring in how we live our day to day lives.

"We could do things like that together if you want; it would be a great way for us to get to know one another and we could watch each other's back. I also happen to love going for nature walks, anything the light touches is so magnificent... You don't have to give up something you love because of me. We can work through this.... Together." I smile as I watch his posture return to normal. He reminds me of a soldier walking to battle, with his broad shoulders, strong arms, thin masculine waist and his back as straight as a needle. He's even wearing a camo shirt which reinforces the look.

"You'd go hiking with me?... I've never done that before.... I mean gone for walks with someone else. I usually go alone. Most of my friends don't enjoy hiking... But you would seriously do that for me?" He looks excited like a kid at Christmas. *Has he seriously never gone hiking with anyone before?*

"Sure. Why not. We would both be doing something we enjoy. We'd be able to keep each other safe and get to know each other. It's the perfect solution." It could be really fun to spend some time with him outside in the sun.

"You know what Kyra, Flick was right, you're a really awesome chick. She couldn't stop raving on about you when she first told me about you. She had nothing but kind words to say." My happy mood plummets. *Of course she would say nice things. Flick is amazing. The best friend a girl could ask for.* I knew we would have to talk about Flick eventually but I was hoping we would get to know one another a little first. I suppose we do need to discuss it though. Especially what we are going to do when it comes to work. We all work together and I don't want to risk losing my friendship with Flick.

"I feel terrible about what has happened. Did you know that she has had a crush on you for like.... months? Then the day after you guys finally go out on your first date, she introduces you to me and... well, you know the rest." I feel heartbroken for my friend and shame washes over me. I unintentionally stole the man she has been crushing on for ages. *If I could take away her pain, I would.*

"Meeting you was just bad timing, no offence. I knew that Flick liked me, she used to stare at me any chance she got. I knew it was only a matter of time before she asked me out. She is hot...and smart and funny. I used to check her out too." He says sheepishly. We turned the corner and I glance over at Duncan, he has this dreamy look in eyes and I instantly feel worse. *Did he really like her too, have I ruined a love match?* Trying to clear my thoughts, I recall something Flick told me.

"She said that you were too intimidated to ask her out." He laughs out loud at my statement.

"Ha-ha. Yeah that's what I told her, but seriously Kyra, look at me. Without sounding too arrogant, have you seen my face? It's not hard for me to get women; and you've seen Flick, she is a hard 10, what type of man would I be if I grovelled at her feet asking for a date? That's not me. It was better that I waited and let her approach me." His eyes dart towards me for a moment before he gazes back at the path before us. *So he did like her enough that he thought about asking her out. He is only with me because he has no choice.*

Trying to lighten my sudden downer mood, I joke. "You are seriously up yourself Mr...." It dawns on me then that I have no idea what his last name is. *I'm bloody irreversibly linked to the man and I don't even know his full name.*

"Memphis...Duncan Memphis and you are?" *Oh, it's Mr Bond now is it? Down to the British accent and all.* The way he says it has me giggling like a fool and my sombre mood vanishes. I think he may have sensed where my mood had shifted and was trying to lighten the moment. Stopping in my tracks, I stick out my right hand and say, "I'm Kyra...Kyra Reynolds, it's nice to meet you Mr Memphis." He smiles and gently grasps my hand, I will never get over the sensation our touch creates. It feels so good and makes all the hairs on my body stand straight up, as a tingling feeling washes over my body. It revives me and makes me feel brand new. My body wants to take a step forward into his embrace and I have to physically stop myself from moving. The urge to connect with him is intense. Tearing my eyes away from our hands, I peer up at his face and see that he too looks as if he is trying to stop himself from moving. It's so strange, we barely know each other but this pull is incredible. I feel like we know each other on a spiritual level that I cannot explain. Clearing his throat, he leans forward.

"It's a pleasure, Miss Reynolds." He moves my hand towards his lips and places a soft kiss on my knuckles. "And Kyra?... just for the record. Although us meeting wasn't the best timing, I'm glad it happened." I'm shocked into silence. *I thought he wanted to be with Flick.* "I have always felt like something... Some part of me was missing, it was a lonely place. The day I met you, it felt like that missing piece had been found and now I feel a sense of belonging. I know that sounds corny but…that's how I feel." His lips lingered on my knuckles while he spoke and he leaves them there for a moment longer, before turning my hand slightly and grasping it in his own.

Without another word he continues to walk down the path towards Willows. Pulling me with him. He has rendered me mute, I don't know how to respond. *Wow! That was… I don't even know what that was, but it was beautiful.* I still feel bad for Flick, that will never change. Though without knowing, Duncan has soothed the shame I was feeling.

I learn quite a lot about my Soulmate on our short walk to Willow's house. He's a huge fan of science fiction films, just like me. This is really awesome because if we ever get the chance to watch a movie together, I know he won't get bored with my choices like Flick did. She hates watching them with me and because of that I always end up watching a romance film just for her. *I would rather pull out my own teeth, than sit through a sappy romance movie… but for her I would watch a marathon of them.*

Along with the rock climbing and the hiking, Duncan also likes to play rugby and basketball. He even challenged me to a game of one on one. We will have to see about that one though, with everything that's going on I don't think I will have the time, not now anyway. Duncan has travelled everywhere and lived in so many different countries. The stories he told me of all his adventures, were both exciting and terrifying. I found out we both have an inkling for foreign food, some of his favourites being Chinese, Italian, Indian and Thai, which is fantastic because I love all of those too. He expressed his love of books, mostly self-help and motivational genres, loving facts more than fiction. *Not my kind of book but each to their own.* We were so engrossed in our conversation, discussing a movie we'd both seen and enjoyed, that we almost walked right past Willow's house. I came to a halt as we finished off our conversation.

"Ha-ha mine too, Boomer would seriously have to be the best character out of the whole series. He's courageous and funny and let's not forget his charming personality. I remember when the movies first came out, I was in Los Angeles at the time and there was a huge line around the corner just to get in. My friends and I couldn't wait to see it and it seriously didn't disappoint." It's exciting to be able to talk science fiction films with someone who's knowledge is as great as mine, we have agreed and disagreed on almost everything.

Standing out the front of Willow's house on the footpath, I almost forget that we are still in the human realm. If I hadn't noticed the absence of the purplish glow of Zagoria, I would have gone up to the door and probably made a fool out of myself to the people who live here in this realm. Turning to Duncan, I am about to tell him to fade out when I notice the worried expression on his face.

"Hey it's ok, trust me, she won't bite. You're safe with me, I promise" Speaking as soothingly as I can, I put my hand on his shoulder for reassurance.

"Thanks but I'm not afraid of her. I'm just concerned that's all...How will we be able to trust what she says, especially if she hasn't dealt with this sort of thing before? And what if she has withheld vital information already. I just don't want to put you in a difficult position. I can tell that she is really important to you and I don't want our questioning to jeopardise your relationship with her." *I love that he is worried about my relationship with Willow but I'm not. I trust her with my life.*

"I trust her wholeheartedly, I always have and always will. If she hasn't dealt with this before, we will explain it to her. Especially about what happened this afternoon, how you saved my life and how it occurred. Then after we have finished here, we could go see your Elder and he can explain the rest to me. Once I have all the information, we can work out how we are going to operate together... Nothing to worry about now, one way or another we will get the answers we need to make this work." I offer him a small smile, hoping to soothe his anxiety and reaffirm that everything will be fine. We stand on the footpath in silence for a moment, processing what I have just said, then suddenly Duncan lifts his eyes from the ground and begins rapidly searching the area around us, while instinctively taking a step closer to me.

Quietly he says, "Kyra, can you feel that? Or is it just me?" Comprehension on what he says takes only a moment and just like that, I snap into battle mode. My stance becomes stiff and I'm ready for anything but my senses tell me it's not an attack that's coming, it's something else. *I sense sadness and sorrow, it's all around us, but where? What is it?* Swinging my head from side to side, I try to pinpoint its location. I can't get a lock on its position though. Someone or something is hurting but I can't find it. *What's going on?*

While my eyes continue to roam the vicinity I quietly respond, "I feel it too but where is it coming from?" Duncan doesn't avert his gaze, even for a second. He is on high alert. Without a word he reaches for my hand, gripping it tightly. Through the bond I can feel his worry, he's not concerned about himself though, he's worried about me. I wonder if he is afraid something is coming for me and that he won't be able to protect me from it. *Strange... I didn't know that there were others that could sense beings like me. Has he always been able to sense them around him or has it been passed onto him through me?*

"Duncan... hey look at me..." I reach out and rest my hand on the side of his face, encouraging him to look at me. "...It's going to be alright, we are together and I can protect us, there is no need to worry."

"You don't have to protect me Kyra, I have enough strength to protect us both. I'm not just your soulmate, the bond between us magnifies our pre-existing abilities and also gives us some new ones, the resources to help keep each other safe. We give each other extra strength and power just by touching, we are stronger than ever before as long as we are together." *Oh, I didn't see that coming. Is that why he grabbed my hand just now, to gain strength for whatever was coming? I wonder how heightened my abilities will be.* "I don't know what it is we're sensing and I don't really feel like finding out, let's just fade and go see Willow, before whatever that is makes itself known." Indecision floods my senses as I look up at my mate beside me, his eyes are darting all over the place, keeping an eye on our surroundings.

I'm torn, I want to know what this being is that imparts such bleak emotions but I'm also aware that Duncan and I are not ready for a confrontation. *We don't even fully know what we are capable of.* Coming to the conclusion that it would be best to take the non-confrontational route, I say, "You're right, let's go." Still holding hands, we fade out together.

We are immediately thrown into chaos, throngs of people are gathering around Willow's doorstep. Some are crying, some are whispering and others look downright angry. There are so many people I can't even get a good look at the front of her house. Whatever is going on can't be good, Willow hates crowds, she will only tolerate them if it's for a party. *This sure doesn't look like any party I've ever been to.*

I notice Elder Kit standing to the far left of the masses and decide he is probably the best person to talk to right now. I head in his direction, pulling Duncan behind me.

"Elder Kit.... Elder Kit..." I shout as I weave us through all the people, waving my hand in the air, trying to get his attention. He must hear his name being called over the noise because he looks up in my direction. He has a surprised expression on his face once he realises it's me. I get the impression he knows what's going on and I'm probably the last person he was expecting to see here. *I suppose I was bedridden only a few hours ago.*

"Good evening Your Highness, you are looking much better. I heard you were still quite ill?." He bows his head as he speaks. *Even with all the craziness going on around us, he is still so formal.*

"Yes I was feeling quite unwell but thank you, I'm feeling much better now...Elder Kit... What's going on? What's with all the people?" As the words leave my mouth I feel his regret, he tears his eyes away from mine and looks towards the house. There is something very serious going on and he looks hesitant to tell me. Whatever it is though, he knows he has to tell me. I am the Princess and he can't keep things from me. I can sense that this is more to protect me, than him not wanting to tell me. Unease builds within me as he shakes his head and turns back to face me. I'm instantly on high alert the moment we make eye contact. *The words I am about to hear are not going to be good.*

"I'm sorry to be the one to tell you this Your Highness, but Elder Willow was taken earlier today by the Darkness."

I stand there in stunned silence. I can't move, can't feel. *Willow... Taken... by the Darkness... How?...* It feels like I stand there in shocked silence for hours, before I fall to my knees. Tears soundlessly roll down my face as I try to process this information. They went after Willow, the one thing I didn't protect, shouldn't have to protect. *She was taken because of me; they knew how close I was to her. I haven't hidden how close we are. How much I care about her, I love her like I would a mother. Because of this, they have taken her! I will never be able to forgive myself if they hurt her. This is all my fault. I should have insisted she stay at my place last night, if I had, this never would have happened.*

Duncan falls to his knees beside me, taking me into his arms, holding me tight while I cry. Seemingly oblivious to the turmoil rolling around in my head, Elder Kit continues to speak. Offering little comfort to the emotions going haywire within me.

"We're sorry Your Highness, I know how close the two of you are." *Way to rub salt in the wound Kit.* "We have search parties out everywhere looking for her. We can confirm it was a crawler who took her but as of yet we are unable to locate what direction they went."

"This can't be happening... Fuck I hate him! Why did he go after her? Why didn't he just come after me?" I look to Duncan as I speak, gazing into his eyes. I don't know why, maybe I am hoping he will have all the answers. I'm disappointed as he shakes his head confused and whispers, "Who baby, who do you hate?"

Through my tears I sob, "The Prince, Duncan... The fucking Prince! He took the one thing that means the world to me, other than yourself. You won't understand Duncan, Willow isn't just an elder to me, she is my family and he took her to get to me...This is all my fault. She could die because of me, because of this war. If she dies I will never forgive myself." *When I die, I get reborn, Willow doesn't have that opportunity, if she dies, she is gone forever.* I feel Duncan's lips move against my skin, he's saying something but I'm too far in my own head to understand what it is.

Oh Willow, I hope you are ok. They better have not laid a finger on you because I'm going to find them and when I do, I'm going to rip them apart. Duncan tenses as violence, like I've never felt before, replaces my devastation. I am filled with an overwhelming urge to kill, kill anything and everything that gets in my way. I will stop at nothing until I have Willow back. My tears have evaporated and I move to stand up, but Duncan's hold on me tightens and I cannot move.

"What are you doing? LET ME GO!" Frustrated, I growl in his ear as I fight his hold on me. *I must find Willow before anything happens to her. Soulmate or not, he will not stand in my way.* Somewhere deep down, I understand that I need to calm down but every nerve in my body is on high alert and screaming at me to do something. To rescue Willow, avenge her and bring her home, where she belongs. I try as hard as I can to break free from his grasp but it's proving difficult. He is just too strong. It should be easy for me to break free as I'm stronger than most Zagorian's, it's part of who I am, part of being the Light Princess. *It must be the bond giving him this strength. Stupid bond giving him help, when I need him to let go.*

"Kyra, you need to calm down! I'm not letting you go anywhere while you have so much rage inside you, I can feel it. So stop trying to fight me and relax." As if to back up his words he tightens his grip on me and I feel as if my bones are going to snap. I won't give up though, I cannot explain it but I have to get free, I must find Willow. It's the only thought I have and I can't sit here on the ground and do nothing while the crawlers have her.

Crawlers are nasty vile things. If one was to ever cross your path, you'd know it. They are skeletal creatures that have black ooze covering their entire form, they have razor-sharp teeth inside the wideset mouth and can unlock their jaw and swallow you whole, just like a snake. The ancient texts also believe that they are not smart creatures, they've been known to act first think later. Around the time the order of light was being established, we came across one, it jumped from the bushes and without warning, ate a solider right in front of us. One moment the soldier was there and in two seconds flat, he was gone, it was terrifying. I've dealt with a few of them since then and have had to develop a unique style for killing them. They are easier than other dark creatures to locate though, due to their distinct smell. They smell like burnt rubber. *If one of these things have Willow, we must find her immediately. I can't even think about what they may be doing to her.*

With that thought, my attempts to escape Duncan's hold become more frantic and I growl in warning, "Duncan, I swear, if you don't let me go right this second, you're going to force me to do something I'm going to regret." I'm fighting with all my might but he's just too strong, I can't escape his hold. Assessing my options and taking stock of everyone around me, I come to the realisation that the only person close to me is Duncan. Kit has stepped away to give us some privacy, which means we are the only two in the area. I'm glad for this as there is a way I'll be able to get out of his grasp but it's going to take a hell of a lot of energy to do it and could potentially harm someone who isn't as strong as us.

Duncan gives me a smug smirk and says, "Give it your best shot sweetheart, I'm not letting you go until you calm down." He must sense that I'm not making an idle threat because as he says the words, his hands around my wrists get even tighter, he knows that whatever's coming is going to be big. *Yeah you better hold on buddy. Shit is getting real now.* Offering up my own little smirk, I quit struggling and close my eyes, calming my body and focusing on the one thing only I can do, what I was born to do. *Protect those who cannot fight, defend the light as it shines bright, the darkness cannot win this fight.* The power swells deep within the pit of my stomach and I feel it burning as it builds. I feel it surging and just before I let it take over, I turn my head and whisper in his ear, "You asked for it." As the last word leaves my mouth, the power of the sun takes hold and Duncan is thrown back with a whoosh.

"I am Princess of the Light, protector against the darkness. DON'T try and stop me from protecting those who are in need, it's my duty. Willow is in grave DANGER and I will stop at NOTHING, until she is found! So get out of my way." With the power of the sun coursing through me, my voice is much louder than I intended and everyone hears my outburst. It brings me no pleasure when I have to pull rank and highlight my authority to those around me but in times like this, it's good to have it. Duncan may be my soulmate and now have some of my abilities, but I am still in charge here and that isn't going to change. Due to my outburst, the people milling around the house realise they are in my presence and stop to bow their head toward me. *Fantastic!*

To avoid more unwanted attention I look over at Duncan and see sadness and anger directed at me. He is sitting awkwardly next to Elder Kit, holding his arm. I feel remorse while I look into his eyes. *Just a teeny-tiny bit... I understand that he doesn't want me to go but he must know how important this is to me. I love Willow with all that I am and I know that going out there to find her means putting us in harm's way but I can't just sit here and hope that the search parties find her. Willow is in trouble and I will do everything in my power to rescue her.*

Shaking his head, he brushes himself off and gets up, stomping his way over to me. "You had to make a big spectacle, didn't you? You couldn't just calm down for ten fucking minutes so we could discuss this situation? Whatever, it doesn't matter. You broke my elbow when you lit up like a Christmas tree and now I need you to heal me...

Fuck, it hurts like a bitch!" *Oh, he's mad? Seriously, what did he expect?* Extending his hand towards me, he huffs impatiently, waiting for me to heal him. I know that our touch will take his pain away, so I reach out to touch him. Just before our fingers do connect though, I quickly withdraw my hand. *I know it's childish but I'm mad at him too and he can't just order me around like that, especially not in front of all these people. He should have let me go when I asked, instead he chose not to. He can just deal with the pain for a little while. Maybe he will listen to me next time.* He notices me withdrawing my hand and I can see it's pissing him off. He lifts his head to look me dead in the eyes and gives me one hell of a glare. *If looks could kill I would be incinerated on the spot.*

"Kyra, what are you doing? Give me your hand, or I'm going to..."

"Do what Duncan?" I interrupt him. "What are you going to do?... I asked you to let me go and you didn't, I warned you that something like this might happen. You were too stubborn and confident that you were stronger than me, to listen... And guess what? That backfired on you, so I think you should have to suffer the consequences of your pig-headedness for a little while."

How embarrassing, we are having our first fight and it's in front of all these people. Isn't this just fantastic. I need people to respect me and have faith in my judgement and abilities and with Duncan arguing and questioning me in front of them, it's mortifying, and I am so pissed that this is even happening. Duncan is making me look weak.

"My actions? Are you for real right now? I've been suffering for days because of something you did. You nearly killed both of us as a result of going to the Cerberus nest. I wasn't letting you go just now because I was trying to stop you from putting us in danger, again. I just wanted you to wait one second so we could talk about it and come up with a plan so we didn't wind up dead. Remember Kyra... If you die, I die... And I don't want to see either of us dead. I would like to have a long, happy life with you but you just couldn't give me that moment could you? You're unbelievable you know that. Bloody unbelievable and you call me pig-headed."

"I'm sorry for how you suffered, I really am. You have to believe that if I had known what the consequences were, I would've been more careful. If I had known that touching you would heal me and stop all that pain, I would have come to you. But don't you dare throw that in my face, because I DIDN'T know. YOU did though, YOU knew that if you came to find me, you could stop both our suffering and you didn't. You decided to stay away and prolong our suffering, not me. I almost died because you were taking your time, coming to terms with everything. I may be at fault right now but you are in no way innocent." The last few words end in sobs. I'm crying again, for the unfairness of this situation, for the unstable ground that Duncan and I are on and for Willow out there somewhere, only Zagoria knows what is being done to her or where she is. Overcome by so many emotions, I turn around and run from the crowd. I never wanted my subjects to see me cry, crying is interpreted as a sign of weakness. Elder Kit has always said, "Never let anyone see you cry. Crying can be seen as a weakness and you need to be stronger than that. Your people need to trust that you are strong and that you can protect them." He would always ask me during training, "Are you strong Kyra?"

I'd ran about a kilometre down the road before I hear, "Kyra! Hey Kyra, will you just stop please?" I ignore him and continue to run down the street. I can't stop, if I stop I think my body will collapse from all the chaos inside me. Within a few minutes though Duncan is grabbing my right arm, exactly where the Cerberus bit me. It's still quite tender, even though it's fully healed and I yelp from the sudden pressure. I come to a stop and turn around to face him. "Shit, I'm so sorry. I forgot about the bite. Are you ok?" Not making eye contact with him I just nod my head, feeling ashamed for everything that just happened, what all those people witnessed.

I'm looking towards the road, watching the cars drive past, when I feel his fingers gently cup my chin. He lifts my face to meet his and says, "Hey... Don't hide from me. It's ok to be vulnerable around me. I'm your partner in this now but we need to learn to work together. I know you have always done this on your own but now you don't have to... And I'm sorry about before too, I didn't mean to get mad at you in front of all those people. I was just afraid that you were going to run off and do something impulsive without thinking it through properly. I don't want to see you get hurt again."

I take a second to process his words. *He's right. We do need to start working together and including the other in our decisions... This is going to take work.* "I understand your fears Duncan, I really do. I have them too, but Willow is out there somewhere and I have no idea where, I don't even know where to start looking. I'm terrified that something bad is going to, or has happened to her and it's all my fault. I agree that we need to start working together and it may take some time but all I can see is Willow locked up somewhere, scared and alone." Without saying a word, he reaches forward and grabs me from behind the head, gently pulling me to him. He rests my head on his shoulder and wraps his arms around me, holding me in a loving embrace. I lift my arms and wrap them around his waist and instantly feel safe. *It's so strange... How an embrace can make you feel so protected.*

I know tears continue to roll down my face without my consent, which only makes Duncan hold me tighter. Crying won't bring Willow back, actions will and I must find her but at this very moment it feels so nice to be comforted. "It's going to be ok; we will find her and I mean WE because wherever you go, I go too." *What? He can't come, he will get hurt.* I know we just spoke about doing things together but an intense fear for his welfare takes hold and I lift my head to argue but he holds it in place. "Oh no you don't, I'm going with you and that's final. I'm either coming with you, or you're not going at all. We ARE doing this together, as a team." Even though I'm totally against it, I smile. I've only known him a few days and he is already driving me crazy.

What fun we are going to have together... so long as we don't kill each other first.

"Fine you can come...but we are doing it my way." I say this firmly and leave no room for argument. He must accept this because he moves my head slightly so he can kiss me softly on the forehead.

"I can agree to that." For a while we just stand like that, holding each other in the middle of a suburban street. I wish we could stay like this forever but unfortunately the world isn't that nice and there are things to be done.

Chapter 12

After I've come down from my burst of power, we head over to the compound. I've never seen so many people here, it feels as if all of Zagoria is on the hunt to track Willow down. People are running in and out of the hanger and people are yelling at others, instructing them to quicken their pace, as the trucks are gearing up to leave.

In all of our history, an Elder being taken by the opposing side has never been recorded. It's not a crime among our people to actually kidnap an Elder, but it should be, it's just not logical to ever attack them. Elders are second in command, I am the only person that would be made priority over them. Those who have taken her have made a serious error in judgement or just don't care about the ramifications, either way, we will ensure they will suffer a fate worse than death.

While all the hustle and bustle is taking place in the hanger, Duncan and I are staring at a map of Sydney in the command post, trying to pinpoint the spot where there has been an increase in crawler activity. Hopefully that will be where they have taken Willow. Duncan is examining the map, following all the little pins that are marked across it, outlining all current crawler movements that have been reported. He moves his face closer, trying to see the location names, written underneath hundreds of these multicoloured pins.

"These creatures come to our work?" Duncan asks this in disbelief, taking a dumbfounded step back from the board.

"Unfortunately yes, by that expression I'm guessing you've never seen them?"

"Never. I work in the building mostly, studding ceilings and stuff like that. It's rare that I'll even leave the site for lunch, we usually just eat up on the floor we're working on... How often do they appear? Because these numbers are huge?" He is shocked and I don't blame him, there is a huge amount of pins on the wall around where we work. Fighting Darkness's minions has become such a normal part of my day, so I'm not really shocked that they are around this particular area. What does shock me though, is the amount of dots in and around where I work.

I didn't realise this was how many the order had been dealing with, and this is only the crawlers. Thinking back to the argument I had with Elder Kit the other day, I feel terrible and foolish for not listening to him. *Why was I not told these exact numbers?* If I had known the extent of the situation, I would have allowed him to assign more warriors around my workplace. *The stats on the board are seriously disturbing.*

"I encounter a minion almost daily, sometimes twice a day and if I'm not at work, they come to my home and try to attack me there. It's become part of my daily activities, so I'm used to it... The crawler stats are all over the place here though and a lot larger than what I was led to believe. I'm going to go see what I can find on the computer." I utter this as I walk away from the board, heading over to the desk in the far corner of the room. Elder Kit must have been in here earlier, going through the files stored in our archives because every tab about the crawlers is open. Stories about their past, present and future, what prophecies have been spoken about them, stats on how many of us they have killed and information detailing locations where sightings and attacks have taken place, are all open on the screen. There is so much data on these vile creatures, hopefully some of it will be useful.

Lost in my own thoughts, I am startled when Duncan says loudly behind me, "Are you kidding me? They attack you daily. What the fuck! I was thinking maybe it's a one-off kind of thing, not every damn day."

"Like I said Duncan, dealing with the Prince's lackeys is just a normal part of my day, what's not normal is how these creatures managed to get through Willow's wards and get close enough to kidnap her. I still can't comprehend how they managed it, especially seeing as Willow can sense the future. How didn't she see this coming? There has been only one other time the Dark creatures have gotten past her ability, it happened many years ago, before my current rebirthing and although I know about the event, I'm not privy to the entire story. I'm extremely curious to find out how they managed it though." When the Dark creatures got past her abilities last time, it was when the last Princess was attacked and we know how well that ended. We say nothing else as I continue to stare at the computer screen, willing it to show me exactly what I need to see, unfortunately though, it doesn't.

Weeks have gone by and there still have been no leads as to where Willow may be, trucks of soldiers have come and gone and not one of them have returned with good news. The order has nearly searched the entirety of Australia, looking for signs of either the crawlers or of Willow but to no avail. It's like they have completely disappeared. To add to my worries, I've had to take an extended leave from work so I can focus all my energies on bringing Willow home. It's not that I mind taking the time off. *Willow is more important*. It's just that Connor and Flick have been asking a lot of questions and there are only so many excuses I can give them. *It's not like I can tell them the truth.*

Honestly, this has gone on far longer than anticipated and I'm so desperate for information that I don't even want to leave the compound. *What if we get word of where they are hiding Willow while I was gone? I want to be here when we find her. I also want to know the details as soon as it's available so that I can personally kill every one of those vile pricks who have held her hostage. I'm going to make them pay.*

Duncan has been here a lot too, although he does have to go to work most days and can only be here in the evenings.

We decided it would be best for one of us to continue to go, otherwise it would raise suspicion. He's become my right-hand man in all of this, giving me advice and helping me to remain positive. It's a hard feat seeing as we have had no news since the day she went missing and my positivity diminishes a little more, with every day she is not found.

"Hey Kyra, come and have a look at this," Duncan calls from the table. I leave my standing post in front of the map on the wall and go over to him. I peer over his shoulder and see the statistics for all crawler attacks for the last ten years, spread out all over the table. This data identifies the townships that recorded attacks in that time, the information is sorted by the lowest to highest amounts of attacks. Dellpond, Darling Harbour and Victors Bay being amongst the highest.

Duncan must have recognised this too because he says, "The last printout we were looking at stated that Dellpond, Darling Harbour and Cossgrove were the townships with the highest amount of attacks, but if we go off this one it says differently. How can that be?" His face scrunches in confusion and I have to admit, I feel a little confused myself. I too, don't understand how that's possible, they are both from the same time period. I riffle through the paperwork spread out on the table and I come across the sheet I'm looking for, another printout of recorded Crawler attacks, though this is only from the last five years. Victors Bay is seventh on the list. That means that in the last five years, the number of attacks significantly decreased.

"How strange, do we have the stats going back fifteen years?" I ask.

He flips through a few piles of papers and pulls out the sheet I asked for. "Here." He says, handing me the file.

"Thanks." I take the piece of paper out of his hand and lay it next to the other two documents on the table. Scrutinising the information side by side, I notice something. *There!* On the last page, depicting data from 15 years ago, it shows that Victors Bay is in the number one spot for the most crawler attacks. *I bet if we were to look even further back, the numbers would be even more substantial.*

Absentmindedly I say, "I think we've been looking in the wrong spot this whole time. We have been basing our searches on the statistics available for the last 5 years, but we should have been looking elsewhere... At a broader view... Hey Elder Kit! Come take a look at this." I call him over without a second thought. *I know I'm onto something and my blood is pumping with excitement.* Elder Kit comes running over from where he was at the entrance of the hanger, he has been coordinating the troops, organising shifts and what tasks need to be completed.

He stops a short distance away and says, "What have you found?" He moves around the table and peers down at the papers before me.

He asses the data with a slight frown on his face and I can see the moment he identifies what we have found. He looks up at us with a raised brow and I rush on to confirm.

"Duncan noticed a discrepancy with the figures on these reports. We previously thought that Dellpond was the spot with the highest amount of attacks, which is correct, if we are going by the statistics from the last five years. However if we look back further, you can see that the information is wrong. Victors Bay in northern Sydney actually holds the title for the most crawler attacks for the last fifteen years... I have no idea how we missed this. Damon and the crew should be notified immediately. We have been focusing our efforts in the wrong location."

Elder Kit nods his head, "I agree Your Highness. I'll send word out to them as soon as possible." He bows as he exits and heads in the direction of the obstacle course. He only makes it a few paces before I stop him with a gentle hand on his arm.

"With no disrespect Commander but sometimes your methods of communicating information can be a bit slow and this new information is of the utmost importance. I really want this investigated now. If you don't mind, I'd like to handle this one."

He offers me a sympathetic smile and says, "Of course Your Highness, It's no problem at all. I know how difficult these past few weeks have been for you. Willow is lucky to have someone who loves her as much as you do."

"Thank you Commander," I reply absentmindedly. My thoughts are flying in a million different directions. Damon needs to see this information and he needs to see it now; especially if we are correct, this could make all the difference. I feel as if we've been looking in the wrong place this whole time. *If these numbers are correct, Victors Bay surely is the area where the crawlers attacked most frequently. This is where we should be searching every nook and cranny; not Dellpond.*

The attacks are further apart than those of more recent times, nonetheless that's where we should be looking for Willow. Now that this information has come to light, I feel an intense pull towards this location. It grows in urgency as the moment's tick by. Thinking fast, I gather up the numerous papers and run out of the compound, unthinkingly leaving Duncan behind. There are throngs of people milling around, even though it's been weeks since she was taken, we have not slowed down our efforts to find her. While making my quick dash through the grounds, I try to come up with a solution to get this information to Damon as quick as possible.

A wisp is fast, but so is a dragon. Though neither will portray all the information that Damon requires... How can I get this information to him as quickly as possible... Think!... oh I know, a Butterfly! They are a beautiful and mysterious creature, that cannot only pass on the message but can show the receiver everything the sender wants them to see. They peer into our mind's eye and gather up all the information that is required to convey the correct message. I quickly run over to the garden and look for any signs that a butterfly is near.

After searching for what feels like an eternity with no success, I raise my hand to the sky and will one to me with my mind. Within moments, one lands on the tip of my index finger. In just a few mere seconds, the information is transferred and all the data, the findings, everything we need Damon to know is now not only within this butterfly but every butterfly in the world. With a little wave of my hand the creature takes flight. Every butterfly in the world will now be looking for Damon and once he is found, a butterfly will come to me with his reply.

After watching the butterfly fly off into the bright mid-afternoon sun, I turn around and head back towards the compound. I don't make it very far though. After only taking what must have been half a dozen steps, a butterfly flaps in front of my face, perching itself on the end of my nose. I am instantly assaulted with thoughts and images, a tiny echo whispers in my head, "Damon has been found and will head up to Victors Bay as requested but he wishes to leave some troops behind in Dellpond. He believes there are a few more locations that need a second look. The rest will redeploy up to Victors Bay and search the area." After offering the butterfly my response of agreeing to Damon's request, the butterfly flaps its beautiful wings and flies away. *Please let me be right and we find Willow in Victors Bay.*

The next morning, as I hop out of the shower I almost feel like a new woman, my skin is refreshed and positively glowing. I haven't felt this clean in days. *Well weeks if I'm being honest.* If it wasn't for Duncan telling me that I was starting to stink, I wouldn't have even taken a shower. He practically threw me in the bathroom, locking me in.

Since Willow was taken three weeks ago, I haven't really been taking care of myself. I don't care for food and I've barely slept, I've also found myself abusing the connection between Duncan and myself. I have uncovered a little trick that when I feel like I'm about to die from starvation, I can reach for Duncan through the bond and get that spark of life, to make my body feel fulfilled. It's wrong of me to use him like that but I can't help it.

The Elders have refused to let me help out on the field, even though I have the higher authority and the look on Duncan's face when I try to push the subject makes me change my mind because it's not just me anymore, I have to think of him now too. *If I die, he dies.* That makes going into any situation unprepared completely out of the question and the whole situation has me torn and my stomach in knots. Every time I even think of food I want to puke.

Shaking my head to erase the depressing thoughts, I quickly dry my hair and throw it up in a high ponytail before putting on a clean pair of jeans and a shirt. Duncan forced us to go back to my place this morning, saying that I seriously needed to grab a fresh change of clothes. It wasn't until we got here and he shoved me in the bathroom, threatening to wash me himself if I didn't cooperate, that I realised it was just his excuse for getting me to leave the hanger. *I must say though, I do feel better after a shower, so I might even thank him later.*

Stepping out into the hallway I hear water running downstairs, he must be having a shower in the spare bathroom. *Good because he was starting to smell too.* I chuckle at the thought and feel my stomach rumble. *I'm actually feeling hungry!* I decide to utilise this time and see if I have any food in the pantry that's either still in date or at least edible. Seeing as I haven't been here in weeks, I'm guessing that all the food in the fridge will be well and truly off by now. I walk down the stairs and as I reach the bottom step, I notice Pixie waving to me from outside my lounge room window. Sauntering over I open the window to let her in.

"Good morning Your Highness, we have missed your presence around the manor. We hope you are well. We wanted to inform you that there were no new attacks while you were gone, the barrier still stands strong and true. Have a lovely day Your Highness." And with that, she turns and flies away, before I have the chance to say anything. *No new attacks, well that's a good thing I guess.* Closing the window, I turn and head for the kitchen, hoping I can find something that will relieve this hunger.

I'm searching through the pantry, trying to locate something that isn't going to give me food poisoning. *There seems to be a lot of canned goods in here but not much else.* Without warning I feel a hard body collide with my back and the air leaves my lungs with an Oomph! Duncan runs into me from behind as he walks inside the pantry.

"Shit... sorry, I didn't think I'd find you in here. I... ah... just came to find something to eat." He says a little caught off guard.

"It's alright, I'm hungry too," I say sheepishly. *Why do I feel so nervous all of a sudden? It's not like we haven't spent almost every day together for the last three weeks.* Perhaps it's because I'm in a small pantry cupboard with the guy my body has only recently awakened for. It's strange, I haven't thought of anything but Willow for the past three weeks, except at odd moments when images of Duncan from my recent dream pop into my thoughts. Not that I mind, it's a welcoming distraction but sometimes these thoughts make it hard for me to look at him; and right now he is so close to me that I can feel the heat radiating off of him. I smell hints of my shea butter and oatmeal body wash underneath the intoxicating smell of his cologne. It's putting my body on edge, it's so arousing. I can feel his warm breath on the back of my neck and I back up with little though and press my back against his front.

I can now feel the full warmth of his skin as it makes contact with mine. We are pressed together from our fingertips to knees and my head is tilted slightly to the left, allowing access to my neck. I feel a rush of warm air on my exposed skin as Duncan breathlessly questions, "Ah...Kyra... what are you doing?" I'm too lost in the feel of him to reply and I push up against him even more. Without warning, he grasps my biceps to hold me in place and leans down to whisper in my ear. "If you keep moving your hips like that, I will not be responsible for my actions." I shiver at his words and he slowly takes my earlobe into his mouth and sucks on it hard. My knees turn to jelly and I'm finding it hard to stand, I hadn't realised until this moment that I was moving my hips against him. How odd, it wasn't until he said it that I became aware of it.

Turning me around, he looks deep into my eyes for just a moment before grabbing me behind the head. He pulls my face to meet his and when our lips touch it's like fire and ice. All of my built-up frustration pours into the kiss and I wrap my arms around his neck, pulling him closer. I never want this kiss to end. In response to my eagerness, he backs us up, until my back hits the wall and leans his torso into mine. I can feel his hardness on my thigh as he licks my lips and I gasp in shock from the sudden sensations that wash over me. Duncan takes advantage of my surprise and his tongue enters my mouth, slowly massaging mine with his own. I'm distracted with the kiss as his big hands slide down my arms to my waist and then to my ass.

In one swift movement he cups me, lifting me off the ground and instinctively I wrap my legs around his waist. I'm out of breath and my panting is to the point of embarrassment but I gently pull away and put my hands on either side of his head, tilting his face to meet mine. Daring a quick look into his eyes, I can see the same desire, devotion and longing that I feel for him every day reflecting back at me. Emotions that have been with me since the moment we shook hands, a feeling I never want to lose.

"In this world filled with darkness, be the light." He whispers this just before I claim his mouth once more. Wanting him, needing him to relieve this longing that has been building up within me. Suddenly, like a bucket of ice water has been dumped over my head, I pull away.

Darkness? Oh my gosh! How could I have forgotten? We shouldn't be doing this. It's not the right time. We have other pressing matters that need our attention, we need to find Willow. It's been weeks and we still haven't found her; she needs my entire attention.

"What are we doing?" I question out loud as I push away. I need to regather my thoughts, I need to think and I cannot do that while his mouth is on me and I am wrapped around him like a boa constrictor. *Oh gods his mouth, the fullness of his lips, it's such a welcome distraction. I want to get lost in the taste of him forever, but we have to find Willow.*

"We're doing exactly what we both want to be doing," he whispers as he forces my lips back to his. He stumbles a little and manages to knock a few cans off the shelf, making a loud bang as they hit the floor. He quickly regains his balance and we are once again lost in the fire of our desire. We are so wrapped in each other, it's almost like we have become one, not knowing where one of us ends and the other begins. Two souls linked together for all of eternity to make one.

Duncan pulls away mid-kiss to trail kisses down the side of my cheek, moving lower till he reaches the side of my neck. I love how he sucks on the skin there and I instantly feel warm all over. I push my hips forward to meet his, needing to feel any kind of friction. His lips are doing all sorts of crazy things to my libido and I need him closer. I tighten my grip on his waist with my thighs and run my fingers through his unruly hair, encouraging him to bring his mouth back to mine. Images of us tangled together on the floor run through my mind and Duncan must have had the same thought because moments later we are lying on the ground with Duncan braced on his hands above me.

We make eye contact briefly, before hands are moving franticly, trying to pull at each other's clothes. *I want him, need him. I need to feel his bare skin underneath my fingertips.* I'm desperate and impatient for it and without any warning, I'm rolling him over so I can straddle him. I can feel his hardness against the crease in my ass when I reach for the hem off my shirt and suddenly freeze. Nausea begins to roll deep in the pit of my stomach and I know I'm not sick. This feeling only comes from the darkness. *Seriously... you had to come now?*

Chapter 13

"Something's coming," I exclaim breathlessly...

"Mmm... I hope so." Duncan clearly isn't paying attention to what I'm saying, as he creates small circles with the tips of his fingers along my thighs.

"No Duncan... Stop... Concentrate. There's a creature nearby... a dark creature... and it's heading this way... Shit... it's getting closer fast. We have to hurry, we need to fade out." I say this as I get to my feet and the shimmer happens instantly, my body is settling into my realm as I turn into the beacon of light that I was created to be. Without another word, I take off down the hall away from the kitchen and I'm almost through the lounge room that leads to the front door, when Duncan fades in. He is staring at me wide-eyed and I hold my finger to my mouth, silently communicating for him to be quiet.

Conjuring my sword, I run through the lounge room and out the front door, pausing on the edge of my porch. I look out towards my garden, it's still and silent and nothing seems to be out of place. *It's here though, I can feel it.* I startle as Duncan comes to an abrupt halt beside me, I didn't hear him follow me. *I need to get used to him being there. It's logical that he would follow me out, where else would he go? I'm just not used to having someone else around.*

The smell hits us before we can see it, days-old trash that's been left out in the hot sun for too long. *Fuck!* That particular smell only belongs to one underworld being, a creature I never wanted to cross paths with again. A Bubak, a flying scarecrow like creature that has the unnerving ability to cry like a new-born baby. A nasty horrible creature, it likes to trick mothers into believing that their child is in danger.

"How is this possible?" Duncan whispers so quietly I barely hear him.

"I'm not sure." I respond, while assessing the area.

"You're not sure about what?" He looks at me with a confused expression on his face.

Now it's my turn to look at him in confusion. "You asked how it's possible and I said 'I'm not sure.'" I cop another whiff of the vile beast and return my stare towards the space on the other side of my fence. *I know you're out there, where are you?*

"What are you talking about?" He crosses his arms and regards me with an expression that makes me feel like I have gone crazy.

Feeling silly I say, "Never mind" and shake my head, dropping the subject. *Did I imagine him talking?... No, I'm sure he really said it. Why is he denying it?*

While I internally process what just transpired, the Bubak suddenly appears and stops right outside my barrier, staring at us through its dark black eyes. Most beings who try to attack me here at my home will run into the barrier repeatedly trying to get to me but this beast doesn't move an inch, it's smarter than that. I turn my head to the left to seek out my girls, their bright colours will ease my nerves and remind me that everything will be alright.

Unfortunately though, I don't see them. *Huh? Where are they?* Panicked, I run over to the little house in my garden and peer inside the window, I see nothing but darkness. *Where could they be?* Searching the yard frantically, I see a hint of blue in the far-left corner near my rose bushes. *Is that Daisy? What is she doing all the way over there?*

Running over to my roses, I catch a glimpse of Duncan out of the corner of my eye, he seems to be having a staring competition with the beast on the other side of the fence. I'm not too worried, it can't get in but I'm still on high alert. *Why hasn't the creature moved yet? It's seen me, but it hasn't tried to attack at all. Something is off.*

As long as the barrier still stands, we are safe. Upon reaching the beautiful blooming roses, I find all the girls huddled together behind a huge fern.

"Ladies, what are you doing all the way over here? Why did you leave your house?" Their behaviour is worrisome, they never leave the confines of their home. The only time they leave is to give me a message but they scurry straight back once the message has been delivered.

"It's the Bubak Your Highness. They like to…. to eat fairies," All three shiver in unison at this comment as they continue. "… and they have a special ability, the ability to slip through our barriers…" *WHAT!!? Why wasn't I aware of this?* "They are the only beasts who can Your Highness. We have not seen their kind for some time and we fear these creatures." They are hugging each other and you can see the fear in their eyes, they are frightened to the bone, I have never seen them this way before.

I tear my eyes away from the girls and I look out towards the creature. It still hasn't moved. *It can slip through barriers, which is unheard of. If it can truly do what they say it can, why hasn't it done so already?*

"It's going to be alright ladies, I'm here ok, I'll protect you. Please go back to your home and do not leave unless I tell you too. You're safer in there than out here in the open." They silently exchange glances with each other, then look towards the Bubak and lastly at me. They give me a quick nod before scurrying back to their little house on the edge of my garden, slamming the door shut and locking it once they are inside. *If they are scared, maybe we should be too. Not once have I ever heard of a being that can slip through our wards.* The last Princess suddenly comes to mind. *Maybe that is how the beasts got in on the night of her attack, which then led to her ultimate demise.*

Hastening back over to Duncan, I notice he has taken on a more commanding stance. His back is stiff, arms crossed and he is giving the beast one hell of a death stare.

"If only looks could kill," I joke with a small chuckle, as I position myself beside him, my stance taking on more of an attack position than Duncan's. I'm ready for a fight, my legs are slightly bent at the knee and my sword is raised, ready for whenever this beast will make its move.

"Kyra, I really don't think now is the right moment to be making jokes..." He says in a chastising tone and continues on. "You do know what that thing is right?... I remember reading stories about them. Long ago, they were the most feared creatures in our land. It is rumoured that even the Dark Prince had trouble controlling them and if the stories are to be believed, these creatures used to take great pleasure in defying the Prince, going off on their own and causing mayhem wherever they pleased. The Prince of Darkness had very little command over them." He spits the words out angrily as he continues to stare the beast down.

I understand his displeasure but why is he suddenly so angry? Is he angry about what he read about them or is it because a creature from those stories is floating roughly eight meters away? I'm pondering over what he has just said, when it dawns on me that he has read histories on the previous Dark Prince's. I wasn't even aware that such things existed. *How is that I didn't know of their existence? Why would the Elders keep such knowledge from me, but allow civilians access to such precious information? This makes absolutely no sense.*

"Duncan... where did you read such stories?" I'm flabbergastered by the new information and I tear my gaze away from the Bubak and unintentionally, relax my stance and I stare at the man beside me in utter disbelief. *Why would the Elders have such vital information like that written down, yet keep it from me, when it could make a monumental difference to the outcomes of this war. So much has been purposely kept from me and I don't like it.* He looks over at me for a brief second, before returning his eyes to the Bubak.

"Honestly Kyra, now is not the time to be discussing this! You have one of the most feared Dark creatures in all of Zagoria, practically on your fucking doorstep and you want to talk about the hidden books of old?..." *Well, when he puts it that way, it does sound a bit silly.* The feeling intensifies, when Duncan looks over at me briefly for a second time. His face clearly showing that he thinks I have lost my marbles. "..and to top it off, this blasted beast is just standing there. We have been out here for well over ten minutes and it has done nothing other than glare at me. It's seriously pissing me off. Is it going to make a move or is it eventually just going to float away?" Duncan mockingly imitates a floating gesture and I look towards the beast to see its reaction.

A cold sensation hits the pit of my stomach as the creature smiles, watching Duncan flap his hands about. Suddenly the beast lifts its arms and sprays green smoke towards the barrier from the tips of its fingers. Upon impact the wards start to shift and change, looking like acid rain. Dark green drops hit the ground as a large hole is burned into the ward. *This creature doesn't just slip through the wards, it destroys them.* Without a second thought, I'm running as fast as I can down the stairs towards the Bubak. I cannot allow it to step one foot into my yard.

I'm almost at the hole in the ward, when the creature abruptly starts screeching. Instinctively I crouch low and cover my ears, allowing the dreadful beast the opportunity to float inside my wards. It immediately heads straight for the little house at the edge of the garden. *It doesn't even want me; it wants my girls.* Before I can even raise myself out of the crouch position I was in, Duncan launches out of nowhere and jumps, tackling the critter to the ground.

The Bubak doesn't hold back and unleashes its vicious claws, raining down scratches all over Duncan's body. It's grabbing and ripping out flesh with every swing of its mighty arms. Red blood flows on to the grass with every strike the Bubak lands upon him. For a moment I can't move, I'm paralysed by the shock of what is unfolding before me, stunned by the bloodshed. *He's going to die.* Is the thought that crosses my mind, right before I'm hit by another. *I need to help him. I can save him.*

Pulled from my stupor, I run towards them and dive to squeeze underneath the creature and within arm's reach of Duncan. Stretching with all that I have and trying to avoid those deadly claws, I grab ahold of his shoulder. He grunts in agony as the electricity from my touch zips through his ravaged body to heals his wounds. "YOUR SWORD!" He yells at me after a moment. His breaths are laboured both from the physical fight he is in and the intense healing he just endured. Realising what he wants to do, I extend my swords towards him and he grabs it in one hand and in one quick thrust, he plunges it into the floating being above him. The Bubak shrieks in pain and attempts to take a few more swings at Duncan, before succumbing to the wound and erupting into a puff of smoke above us.

"Are you ok?" I pant, as I turn him over to see for myself, not giving him a chance to answer. His clothes are in shreds and his torso is covered in scratches. Most of them have healed, but the deeper ones will take some time.

" I'll be alright, that fucker had worse claws than a cat. These scratches sting like a bitch..." Pain is present in his voice as he looks down at one of the deeper gashes across his chest. "... Thanks for saving me, I appreciate it. Remind me to never go into a fight without a weapon again." He raises his head and gives me a sheepish smile.

"It's my pleasure, plus saving you means saving me too right? It's a win-win for both of us." I rush out an explanation as I start to feel embarrassed. He should know that I would have done it regardless but it's still difficult to admit how I feel about him to his face.

"Are you trying to tell me that you only saved me because it saved you too? Gee, nice to know you care." He huffs as he moves to stand, turning around so he is facing the house, away from me. I can see he is trying to hide the smile that has crossed his face. As he turns, he removes his shirt and rolls it up into a ball, then begins wiping the blood off his stomach. *Yummy... Well minus the blood anyway... Look at them abs.*

"That's not what I meant! You know I would never intentionally let anything bad happen to you. I could never let that happen. I just meant that saving you also saved me too, which was a bonus." I know his tone was joking but I feel the need to explain, regardless of how playful he is being. I raise to stand beside him and wipe the dirt and grass off my skin and out of my hair.

"I know Kyra, I was just teasing." He lifts his head and gives me this ultra-sexy smirk which has my insides quivering. Duncan slowly raises his hand to my face and cups my cheek, setting my skin aflame. I go to take a step closer to him but stop at the last moment and turn my head to the right to look at the little house ten feet away. *I need to go see the girls and let them know that it's safe to come out now and make sure they are ok.*

"I'll be right back," I say as I turn abruptly and head over to the far side of the garden. I chuckle when I hear a groan behind me as I reach the girls; sensing my presence they exit their home and exclaim, "Oh thank you, Your Highness! You vanquished the beast, you both saved us!"

"Ladies, are you ok? I'm sorry that the creature got in." At my words they gasp as one and I turn to see what they are looking at behind me. There is a giant hole in the ward that the Bubak created, a terrifying reminder that there are creatures out there who can actually break through the wards. *We are no longer safe anywhere.*

"We will fix it right-away Your Highness." They do a quick curtsey before rushing back inside their home and a split-second later, green, blue and gold lights start flashing from inside the windows. In moments, the wards begin to crackle and fizz as the gaping hole in the barrier begins to close. They are true to their word, as always. I smile as I head back to the man who is standing at the edge of the garden, watching the hole shrink back into nothingness.

"Those Fairies, they are the ones that make the wards that protect your home, aren't they?"

"Something like that..." I respond, shrugging my shoulders, trying to dodge the subject. Willow warned me to never tell anyone about the fairies and what they can really do. She emphasised the importance, that if someone was to see them and start asking questions, just nod and agree to what they believe is to be true. It's the safest thing for my little protectors and myself. My fairies are special, they are the only ones of their kind who have the power to ensure the barrier remains standing, even after they perish. It will not be able to repair itself once they are gone but it will still stand. *So long as it isn't damaged like it was today.* They are truly my saving grace, my protectors in this world and the next.

Trying to change the subject, I say, "So now that we are not in immediate danger, will you tell me where you found the books of old and all the information you have on the Dark Prince?"

"Kyra, now isn't the right time to talk about this. You, more than anyone should understand that you never know who might be listening. I will tell you, I promise. Just not right now, ok." He motions his head towards my fence to emphasize his point and I can't help but agree with that. *Anyone or anything could be listening.*

"Ok... I can't argue with that.". It's logical to avoid discussing something as vital as this out in the open.

There is a slight pause in our conversation and I take a moment to enjoy the beautiful morning, it is doing wonders for my hyper-aware body. Duncan stands less than five feet away and I want nothing more than to finish what we started before, but we mustn't, we have to report back to the compound to warn the others of the Bubak and the unnerving ability it wields. Duncan turns his gaze away from the fence and stares at me with so much desire and longing that I almost run into his arms but there is also a hesitance that wasn't there before.

"Did you... ah... want to talk about what happened before?" He asks awkwardly as he turns again, this time looking back at the house. He must be remembering what happened in there not too long ago because a sexy smile is taking form on his face and he puts his hands in his pockets, moving his foot around, kicking loose stones that line my pathway. *Is he suddenly shy or is he worried about how I am feeling?*

I decide to ease his mind and say, "It was just a kiss Duncan, what is there to talk about? It was bound to happen sooner or later."

"True... I'm just... we could have..." he stutters as a bright red blush creeps up onto his cheeks. He removes his left hand out of his pocket and begins rubbing the back of his neck. I'm chuckling inside at his awkwardness. He is normally so confident and put together. *This is amusing, watching him sweat.* "Kyra what I'm getting at is, we let our desire for one another get in the way of our better judgment, the situation was getting out of hand and if the Bubak hadn't shown up, who knows how far things could have gone.

I'm not saying that I don't want you because believe me, there is nothing I want more. It's just...we should wait until we are both one hundred percent certain that it's what we want and not just our emotions pulling us in that direction. We have only just begun to get to know each other and if we had sex on your kitchen floor, it could ruin everything we are working towards.

We could never take it back and I am in this for the long haul Kyra, I want a future with you and that does not include our first time together happening in that way. I want it to be special for us and have meaning. We will have plenty of time to be adventurous later." He offers his trademark sexy smirk and all I can do is stand here stunned. *Not in my wildest dreams did I ever imagine those words coming out of his mouth.* He is being cautious and caring and that is the total opposite to how these situations have been previously explained to me. I have heard about guys and how they love to get you into bed, most of the time without even knowing your name. I have no experience in the matter but all the tales I have been told are nothing like what Duncan just said. *Did he just say all of that for my benefit or because he truly feels that way?* So many thoughts are running through my head that I don't know how to process them. I whirl around and face away from him so that he can't see the confusion of mixed feelings and... disappointment on my face.

I agree one hundred percent with waiting. I don't want my first time to be on my kitchen tiles but I'm also disappointed that we have to wait. I burn when he is near, it's almost becoming unbearable. On the other hand, I am totally confused with his reaction to the whole thing. "Do you truly feel this way, that we should wait? I completely agree with you, don't get me wrong.

Having sex on my kitchen floor was not really how I pictured my first time. It's just most guys only think about sex and wouldn't even consider waiting." I say all this as I head for the house. Speaking a hundred miles a minute.

"Did you just... did you just say you're a virgin?" He almost whispers the question. *Oh shit!* I stop dead at the bottom of the stairs leading up to my front door. *Did I just declare out loud that I am still a virgin?* I hesitantly look back; Duncan is staring at me wide-eyed with his mouth hanging open. He is so gobsmacked that all he can do is stare at me.

Shit, how am I going to answer this? "I... um... I didn't intend on you finding out just yet and not like this. But... um... yeah I am." I say sheepishly. Nausea begins brewing in my stomach and it's not the beast type of nausea, I feel like I'm seriously going to throw up. This is the most cringe worthy conversation I have ever been a part of. I'm terrified of how he is going to react to this piece of information.

"How is this possible?" He asks me, with confusion and disbelief written all over his face.

I'm immediately on the defensive, "Well if you must know, I've been a little busy these past few hundred years. I am not like everyone else; I cannot just go around and date whoever I like and not have a care in the world. Have you forgotten the beast we just killed already? I don't have time for a life and I certainly don't keep a safe lifestyle. What the fuck would I do if a creature rocked up when I had someone over? Christ! Not to mention I barely even have time for myself, let alone someone else!" I started off cool and calm but am practically yelling at him by the end. I didn't mean to get so defensive about it, it just sort of happened.

"Whoa, Kyra calm down. If I knew asking you that would get you so worked up, I wouldn't have asked. I'm sorry. It was just a shock, that's all." He closes the gap between us and wraps his arms around me, giving me comfort that I didn't know I needed. The instant his arms wrap around me, calm washes through my body.

"I'm sorry, I didn't mean to get so angry. I don't even know why I did... It's just... I have spent my whole life training to be the saviour of our realms, not one single day has truly ever been my own.

I don't mind though, I know my purpose. I have been created into existence to protect life but it can be lonely. Perhaps that's why fate put us together, it knew that I was lonely, so it brought me you." It must have been the right thing to say, Duncan laughs within my embrace and I lean back to stare into his big blue eyes.

Rising onto my tippy toes I move my face closer to his, I need to feel his lips upon mine. He must understand my need because he leans forward and his lips softly make contact with mine. Soft feather-light kisses, just what I need after our deep conversation and all the craziness with the Bubak. It's sweet and calming, exactly what I need. It's nice to just stand here together with nothing interrupting us, just us taking a moment for ourselves.

Duncan moves his head back and rests his forehead against mine. "I'm sorry destiny has dealt you such a lonely hand but I'm glad that fate has brought us together. You are my mate Kyra and I will do everything within my power to make you happy. You will never be alone again. I will always be here for you, to keep you company, help you fight the Darkness and make sure your needs are taken care of. This includes keeping you focused when there are distractions. Like right now, we should go back to the compound and see if they have any news about your Elder, we have been a while." He takes a step back and kisses me on the forehead, before taking my hand in his and turning to head up the stairs into the house.

Fate may have brought us together, but it is up to us to make it work and I will do everything in my power to make that a reality.

Chapter 14

The hanger is full of life when we arrive back, it's even busier than it was when we left earlier this morning. We walk over to the central command station and Elder Kit has his back to us, talking in hushed tones to an officer. It looks as if they could be arguing about something and just before I fully enter the room, Elder Kit turns around. He's glaring at us.

"WHERE, HAVE YOU TWO BEEN?" He booms so loud in the room, that everyone within the hanger stops in their tracks. *This cannot be good.*

"I took Kyra home so we could shower and get some fresh clothes," Duncan answers before I get a chance too. Kit gazes between Duncan and me and I can see that he is getting more pissed off by the second. *What the hell happened while we were gone? I have never seen Elder Kit this pissed before!*

"If I wanted your input boy, I would have asked for it. Who do you think you are, talking to me like that?" He spits out towards Duncan. *What the hell? I have never heard him speak to anyone like that before. This is not our normal Elder Kit.* A shocked expression crosses Duncan's face but he quickly recovers and crosses his arms as he adjusts his stance into a defensive position.

"I am Kyra's mate Elder Kit and I do not appreciate the way you were talking to her. You demanded an answer to a question and I was merely providing that answer. It is my job to protect her, even if it is from one of her own."

I'm touched by Duncan's response but I am completely stunned by Elder Kits behaviour, it is inexcusable. I turn to Elder Kit and with a stern voice that represents my rank and authority, I command, "What the fuck is going on? Elder Kit what the hell has gotten into you? I get that you are an Elder and have certain authorities that others don't have but what you just said was incredibly rude. You asked a question and Duncan was responding as requested and told you where we were!" My voice quite raised at this point, I'm so worked up by his audacity.

If I thought the hanger has gone quiet before, I was wrong. It is so quiet, you would be able to hear a pin hit the floor, I can feel thousands of pairs of eyes on me. Everyone is waiting to see what I will do next, even Elder Kit looks too stunned to answer me. I have never asserted my position over him before and I have definitely never yelled at him. He blinks a few times and clears his throat, before putting his hands behind his back and looking rather ashamed.

"I'm sorry Your Highness, when I arrived at the hanger this morning and was unable to find you both, I feared the worst. Not a soul in this hanger had a clue as to where you both were and with everything that has been going on.... I was just worried. We cannot lose you too Kyra. Please accept my apology, it will never happen again, it was an old man's panic that had me acting in such a way." He looks so much calmer now. He knows we are ok, so he can stop worrying.

"I appreciate your concern but we are ok. We would have come here sooner if it were not for the Bubak that attacked us this morning. So, I too apologise for making you worry. The attack from a Bubak was not something I expected and we discovered something interesting really interesting about it. They have a very unique gift. It has the ability to slip through our barriers... it can create big damn holes in them and get past our protection wards."

"A Bubak? What a very peculiar talent indeed." He says this while walking off towards the computer. I can see from my position in the room that he is doing a quick search in the archives to see what is written there about these beasts.

"Commander.... Commander... they found the nest, requesting back up immediately." All heads turn towards the man running through the front entrance of the hanger. I whirl around and stare at the newcomer and unconsciously grab a hold of Duncan's arm, squeezing tightly. *This is the information we have been waiting for.*

"Where son, where is it?" Elder Kit says eagerly, his computer search suddenly forgotten.

"Victors Bay Sir. Exactly where Her Highness suggested we search." The soldier says this while gesturing towards myself. *They've found it. They've really found it!*

"Then what are we waiting for? You heard the man, they're requesting back up. Let's go! Everyone gear up, we are moving out in five minutes." I shout to the room and anyone within earshot. *Today's the day... We are going to get Willow back.*

About twenty-five minutes later we breach the outskirts of Victors Bay. *What a dump.* By the looks of it, the crawlers have taken over every inch of this tiny little town. Even on the Zagorian plain, it doesn't look like anyone has lived here for a very long time. Rubbish has piled up in the streets, signs have fallen from shop windows and there's broken glass everywhere. *It's like a ghost town here. How can this location be so close by and us not be aware of it?*

We search the streets for what feels like hours and finally locate a group of soldiers gathered at the end of a long road. Sprinting in their direction, we see Damon break off from the group and make his way towards us.

"About time you guys showed up." Damon mockingly looks at his watch then up at me with a smile upon his face. "Your Highness," He says while giving a little bow. *Smartass.*

"Maybe next time you could be more specific with your instructions on where you want us to me you. It took us forever to find you guys, we've been searching the streets up and down for you... So, where is it?" I ask, giving Damon a firm handshake before stepping aside to allow Duncan and the commander through.

"It's below us Your Highness... Sir..." He says as he shakes hands with the commander. "... It's in the underground railway system. A few of our men stumbled upon it earlier today. They sent word out that they had found it but unfortunately, they never returned. Because we were unable to get a full report, we're not really sure how many are actually down there."

"How many soldiers did we lose son?" Elder Kit asks somberly. I hope it isn't a large number. Elders are deeply saddened when any of our people die, especially Willow. She loves life and every life is special and valued, she will detest what is to come, that many of us will die trying to save her. She like myself, hates that people die as a result of our mission. Sadly though, it is what is it, endless battles and suffering to try and keep the peace in a war that seems to have no end.

"Thirteen Sir," he responds, sadly.

"Well, let us go make sure that they didn't die in vain then. Are your soldiers ready to go?" Elder Kit asks Damon as we near the pack, milling outside the railway entrance.

"Of course Sir, we've been ready for hours. We just didn't want to go in there unprepared and possibly outnumbered. In the brief message we received from the soldiers before we lost contact, they think there may be at least five hundred crawlers down there. That would have to be almost the total number of crawlers we are aware of, all congregated in this one location! With a nest as large as this, we believe this is where they're holding Elder Willow. Why else would they all nest in the same location? It's just not logical." He says this last part, while looking at all three of us in turn. *He has a point. It's not logical for them to all be in the same place. Why would they all stay together when they could spread their darkness further by separating?*

Though, with everything that has been happening lately, nothing makes sense anymore. The Cerberus who we fought to the brink of extinction have mysteriously reappeared, an Elder being taken for the first time in history, fate giving me a soulmate, all this strange new information that is arising and now this. Something weird is going on and I have a sinking feeling in the pit of my stomach. I'm dreading to find out what it all means. Maybe the river is dying after all.

Elder Kit breaks into my thoughts. "Indeed son, that is a very large number and is quite disturbing, but no matter. We will take them out soon enough, I just hope Elder Willow is down there. This has been going on for far too long... Your Highness, would you like to take lead on this, or shall I?" He directs this last part at me and I pause before responding. *I'm almost certain that with a nest this size, the first wave of soldiers that enter their domain, most likely won't make it home.* It is a harsh reality but a reality nonetheless and being who I am, I should be the one to lead the group. But this decision is not just up to me anymore, I turn towards Duncan and gaze into his eyes. He offers me a slight smile and I know that he can see my struggle. He can see me warring with my options and can see the question in my eyes. He offers me a slight nod, yes to lead the charge, kill these beasts and get Willow back. He knows through our bond, how badly I want to kill every single one of them that have held her here. *Thankfully he agrees with me.*

"I'll lead us down Elder Kit... Damon is this the only entrance or is there another way in?" I ask this as I look out at the throngs of people, they're standing around a staircase that leads underground.

"We believe this is the only way. We conducted extensive searches of the surrounding areas while we were waiting for you to show up and this was the only one we found."

"Perfect. Ok, so this is what we're going to do, I will lead the first wave of troops down and Damon you will wait roughly ten minutes from when the last of my men have entered and then follow us in with your group. After a further ten minutes, Elder Kit, you will come in to bring up the rear. I will need you both to be on the lookout while we are down there, even though the area was searched, there has to be another entrance. They would not have boxed themselves in like this, they may be known to act first and think later but they are not that stupid." I contemplate the warriors gathered around, we have over a thousand troops here, all crammed into the streets. Every single one of them is willing to do whatever it takes to get Willow back. Just like I will do whatever it takes, to ensure that as many of them as possible make it home safely. "I want roughly two hundred of the soldiers that came here with us to come with me, the rest can wait with you Elder. That should leave you with heaps of protection and be a significant back up, if something should go wrong." I instruct authoritatively. *He won't argue with me when I use that tone and I am in no mood to sit around and bicker, when Willow could be close by.*

"You know I don't need the protection Kyra; I can defend myself. Don't forget who trained you in combat." He exclaims offendedly as he turns away from me to look at the people around him. *That is not what I meant by protection. Gosh, he is so sensitive! Did he not hear the last part I said?*

"That is true but Willow was taken. She may not be as good as you but she can certainly hold her own and they still managed to get her. I couldn't bare to lose you as well. I would rather you have extra protection and be safe than sorry. Plus, like I said, your team will be crucial, if anything goes wrong... Duncan, you're coming with me." I turn towards him and extend out my hand, palm facing up. Within the blink of an eye a fire sword appears. A blade that is an exact replica of my own. It is the same in every way, except it is not an immortal blade. It will kill the beasts like any other blade in existence but it cannot harm myself or any other immortal being. *Not that I'm worried about Duncan trying to hurt me. I know that would never happen but nothing could ever truly replicate my sun sword.*

"Here, you're going to need this... You can't go into a battle empty-handed again." Passing him the blade, he accepts it willingly and swings it around a few times, learning the feel and weight of it.

"Thanks... so we're really doing this?" He says as he rolls his shoulders, moving them from side to side as he stretches out his muscles. I think his question is rhetorical as he knows there is no way I am turning around now. *Also, by the way he is stretching while asking me this question.* Regardless, I answer him anyway.

"You betcha... We are going to kick some Darkness ass!" I offer a cheeky smile before I walk over to the large group of soldiers gathered around. I notice an old rusty car off to the far side which appears to have been abandoned some time ago and jump up onto its roof so I can see the mass of people. "Alright everyone listen up; I will be taking lead on this and I will require roughly two hundred volunteers to accompany me down the tunnels as the first wave. Damon and his troops will follow shortly after and the rest of you will follow with Elder Kit to protect our backs. We need to vigilant down there people, these creatures won't think twice about attacking you, don't hesitate to do the same to them.

Be brave and believe in the light, don't let the darkness scare you, as it will be consuming and will suck your light from you. When it doubt, look for me. I will shine as bright as I can, to help light the way for you... we leave in five minutes, so prepare yourselves. Today we show the Darkness what the light is really made of!" I yell this last part as loud as I can, while holding my sword high in the air for all to see. I'm not going to lie, I'm scared. Not for myself, but for those around me. Crawlers are nasty beings and I foresee a lot of death awaiting us just beyond that staircase. I jump from the car while the soldiers clang about, getting ready for what is to come and seek out Duncan, he must have sensed my worry because he's already sauntering over to me. He pulls me into his arms once I am within reach and holds me tight, igniting a fire that burns in my veins. It's like being zapped by an electric current over and over again. A feeling I have become accustomed too and find myself constantly craving. *A feeling I don't have the time to indulge in right now.*

"Are you ready for this?" I whisper into his chest as I snuggle in a little closer, I'm not ready to let go just yet, I need to feel the comfort of his healing power just a little bit longer.

"I'm ready for it to be over, they never should have taken your Elder. It was a grave error in judgement on their part, what outcome were they trying to achieve anyway? To me, it doesn't sound like something the Prince would do, I thought he was smarter than this. After all, he has eluded you for so many years. I heard rumours, that even the Elders still don't know what he looks like this time around, is that true?" He asks this while stroking his thumb up and down my spine. The rhythm is so calming that I almost forget where we are.

"Yes, the rumours are true. None of us have ever seen him in his current form. We are always hopeful though that if we come across a nest or large quantities of Dark beings, that he will be nearby. Nests are generally formed in locations that are constantly frequented by Zagorian royalty. I have witnessed it myself, in the past they would form nests around my workplace and my home. It made getting to and from work very difficult but in recent years

Elder Willow found a way to stop that from happening." Keeping my arms around him, I lean back so that I can look up at his face. His blue eyes reveal his concern but his unwavering strength is holding strong. *He is such a beautiful man.*

"Willow discovered that peonies have the ability to discourage minions from gravitating around royal powers, such as mine. She didn't go into detail but apparently it works as a type of mind control... Years ago when I moved back to Australia, Willow gifted me a pot plant containing a peony bush. She told me that the peony will bloom for as long as I live and will help dilute that part of my power that attracts the minions. It doesn't stop it completely but does help in attracting so many"

"Well, that is handy, I ...." Battle cries begin to rise within the mass of people around us and cut off whatever Duncan was about to say. We instantly break apart and Duncan quickly glances over at the group before stepping up to me once more. "Time to go." He whispers as he leans down and kisses me on the forehead. He offers me his signature smirk, before moving his mouth to my ear and says, "I know what you must do and I support you a hundred percent but please remember that it isn't just you anymore. We are in this together, I am here to help. So please don't do anything careless." Turning his head, he gives me another quick kiss, this time on the cheek before righting himself and turning to walk over to the entrance to the tunnels. He only makes it a step, when I grab his arm and pull him back towards me. I offer him a cheeky smirk of my own and reach up on my tiptoes to whisper in his ear, the same goes for you, I will follow you anywhere. So just remember that, before you get yourself in a sticky situation." I nip his ear with my teeth and offer a quick kiss of my own to his cheek. I turn with a chuckle and saunter away. *His face was priceless... Ok, let's do this.*

Chapter 15

I'm standing at the top of the staircase that leads down to nothingness. It's so dark I can't see the bottom. They are down there though, I can tell by the smell. Burnt rubber fills my nostrils and the stench is so bad, I almost have to cover my mouth to stop myself from gagging.

Casting my voice loud enough, so everyone above and below will hear my call, I shout, "Protect those who cannot fight, defend the light as it shines bright, the Darkness cannot win this fight." I take one last quick glance at Duncan who stands beside me and take a deep breath. Then I take the first step, leading the troops into the gloom below. The first thing I notice is it's eerily quiet down here, the only noise is our footsteps on the concrete as we move further down into the darkness.

The second is that it's extremely dark in here. Being in my true form allows us to see roughly fifteen metres ahead, but no more. Our soldiers were all provided torches before entering the staircase but looking upon the conditions down here, I believe they will be of no use. Whatever the light touches seems to get swallowed up by the unending darkness.

After what feels like forever, we reach the bottom step and I lift my head, trying to get a grasp on roughly how big the room is. It must be vast as I cannot see the ceiling, just an endless blackness above me. We slowly make our way across the room and pass an abandoned structure that looks to be an old ticketing booth in the centre of the room. Peering inside I can see papers are stacked high on the countertop and I'm instantly curious as to how they got here. *Trains don't run in this realm.* I peruse the top page and notice that they appear to be old newspapers, the headline reads, THE WALL STREET CRASH OF 1929. *How did these get here?* These are papers from the Earth realm.

I lift my gaze to the solider standing closest to me and hold up the paper so he can see it too. Concern floods his features before it is quickly replaced by confusion. A lot of things get transferred between the realms, generally it's houses, vehicles and sometimes even furniture, but nothing like this. *I'll have to tell the Elders about this later.* Putting the paper back down, we walk further into the room, spreading out so nothing can catch us off guard. Ahead of us, I see a tight passageway that appears to lead down to another staircase and stop a good distance away from it.

I wait for everyone else to catch up, when suddenly I hear a scraping sound coming from the direction we are headed in. I raise my sword indicating to everyone to stop and as quick as I raised it, I lower it again, dimming the light just enough so we won't be discovered. In the silence, I can hear the addition of footsteps adding to the increased volume of the scraping, it sounds as if someone is dragging something along the ground.

Suddenly voices join the scrapping sounds and we all hold our breath, trying not to give away our presence. I strain my ears, attempting to hear what the voices are saying. It sounds as if there are two beings in the tunnel and they appear to be arguing.

"Master is not going to like this when he gets here," One of them says.

"That's if he even shows up this time." A pissy voice echos in response.

"Of course, he's going to show up you idiot. This is the master you're talking about."

"Well he didn't show up in Cossgrove, did he? Remember last time when I killed all those soldiers from the order?"

"Did you really expect him to come? He gave you an order and he expected you to execute it. Do you need your daddy to come clap you on the back and say good job everytime you do something he asks?" The first speaker replies mockingly.

"Fuck off... Help me lift this shit, would you?"

"Why are we moving this anyway?"

"Slade wants it moved, that's all I know. Said it would get in the way of his master plans and that..." We miss the end of what is said, as they move further down the tunnels away from us. *Damn it! I wanted to hear what they were saying... Luckily we weren't discovered though.* I wait a few more moments to make sure they're not coming back and then raise my sword again. I wave it around in a circle to attract everyone's attention and without a word, I point it towards the stairs. We carry on with our trek through the room and continue on.

Nausea rolls deep in the pit of my stomach the further we plunge into darkness and the deeper we go, the worse it gets. Damon's missing men said there were hundreds of them down here and they weren't wrong. Without warning a wave of nausea washes over me and I grab a hold of the railing as I near the bottom step to steady myself. The feeling is so overwhelming, I feel as if I'm going to be sick and sure enough, a moment later I'm breaking rank and rushing around the nearest corner. I throw up all over the wall just as Duncan reaches my side.

"Are you ok?" He whispers, while rubbing my back. I am unable to respond as I start to dry heave, usually if it's just the one beast it's manageable but this, this is intense. *There are so many of them down here. I can feel them all.* Once the heaving subsides, I reply with a nod. I don't want to risk speaking and alerting them of our arrival. There is a minuscule chance that they didn't just hear me hurl my guts up. Breathing heavily a few times to regain my composure, I stand up straight and we head back to the troops. It's only now as I look around that I realise the floor is covered in black ooze and the smell has increased tenfold. I still can't see too far around me but this room feels even larger than the last. There also seems to be another tunnel off to the left, so I peer down the long passage and see a flickering light at the end of the tunnel. *They must be hiding down there.*

Before we make our way down the passageway towards the light, I signal with my sword again and instruct the men to conduct a quick perimeter check.

While waiting for them to complete the check and reform the lines, I start drawing in power. These particular creatures are more unpredictable than the last one I fought, they're super strong and will always go straight for the kill. I need to be prepared for anything, even if I'm reluctant to use it because of the after effects.

The burning sensation builds as the power begins to grow within me and suddenly another wave of electricity zips into my veins and intertwines with my power. Looking to my left I see Duncan standing beside me and I feel his hand skimming mine, making me feel alive, as if I'm a burning flame. Gazing towards the flickering light I take a step forward when screams sound from behind me. I swing around towards the noise with my blade in tow and Duncan instinctively moves closer to me. *Well... more like in front of me.*

"Duncan get behind me!" I yell at him over the screams of our comrades. I can barely see a thing in front of us and I can't protect him or fight what's coming when he is blocking my way. Without warning lights shine from up above, illuminating the whole room and I have to blink back the fogginess that clouds my vision. As my eyes begin to focus I notice with horror, that the crawlers took advantage of the situation and have surrounded us. Black bodies line the walls closing us in. *Shit, we have no way out. How did I let them catch us off guard like this?* We're huddled together in the centre of the room and stand back to back as we prepare ourselves to fight. *Where is Damon? He should be here by now!*

Unexpectedly, a gong sounds from somewhere within the room and ricochets off the walls surrounding us. It's so loud that we are left with no option but to cover our ears. As we shriek away from the noise, the Crawlers closest to us press the upper hand and attack. They grab the person closest to them and opening their mouths as wide as they can, swallow the soldier's whole. There is a distinct cracking and crunching sound that reverberates through the room as the solider's bones break, being swallowed into the pit of their stomachs.

People are screaming as they scramble to get closer to the centre of the room, as far away from the beasts as they can. Once the first wave of Crawlers have finished their attack they break away to let the next line of beasts through. *Fuck this! I will not allow for them to pick us off like we are in a line-up.* Getting down on one knee I touch the floor and will the power to me, softly chanting to myself, ".... light shines bright, the darkness cannot win this fight." *One short burst should do it; it shouldn't render me unconscious... I hope.* Duncan has crouched down next to me and whispering just loud enough for him to hear, I say, "Get ready." Duncan quickly stands and passes the message onto the warriors around us. The message is passed on quickly and they collectively glance in his direction. He gestures towards me on the ground and recognition crosses their faces. The soldiers adjust their stance, preparing for what is about to happen and I shoot up into a standing position, letting go of the power within me.

Flailing my arms out wide, a ring of flames pulses out of my being, killing the first line of beasts upon impact and throwing the rest of them back a step. "NOW!" Duncan bellows, as one the soldiers swing their blades, aiming to take off the head closest to them. In no time at all black ooze is glistening all over the place as people hit their desired targets. Dull thuds echo throughout the large room as one by one heads continue to hit the ground. Screeches from those trying to run away add to the noise within the space.

Unexpectedly, someone on the opposing side shouts, "The Master is here; he will save us." However, I am immediately distracted as Damon and his troops leap into the room with a tremendous battle cry. *Finally!* The creatures stop fighting and stand there dumbfounded for a moment, it's as if they weren't expecting this to happen. Their shock wears off quickly though and they continue to fight back, more vicious than before.

The cling and clang of metal on armour and the bang of the gong is all I hear for what feels like hours, that and the thudding sound that is ever present as either heads or limbs consistently fall to the ground. So much death lies around me and I am covered from head to toe in black ooze or some poor soldiers' blood. I look over to Duncan beside me and he looks very much the same. *Too many of us are dying, I need to do something to stop this now.*

"We can't go on like this for much longer. There's too many of them and they're too strong. We will all be dead soon if I don't do something but I need your help." I reach for him and without a word, he takes my outstretched hand, fire and ice ignites within my veins. His touch boosting my inner abilities while I pull as much power as I can from the earth beneath my feet. "Tell the men to get down!" I whisper as I feel the power surging between our interlocked hands.

He drops down to one knee and bellows to the troops around us. Without question they drop to the ground, still stabbing and slashing at any creature that comes within reach. Duncan turns his head to look at me and our eyes lock, I don't miss the worried expression on his face before I close my eyes, focusing on the fire burning within me. I force the flames into a vortex, a spinning tornado of fiery death, preparing to end this madness. Opening my eyes I see that Duncan still has his attention focused on me and I quickly look over his face, searching for the comfort I desire before I unleash the inferno within. Offering him a nervous smile I drop his hand and spread my arms out wide, letting a supernova erupt from my being.

Flames cascade and dance out of me at about a meter in height, parallel with the ground. They slice through any creature in their path, the beasts have no time to react before they are sliced in two.

Collapsing to the floor from exhaustion, I see Duncan reach for me before my vision goes foggy. *I'm completely numb.* He positions himself above me and slowly my sight clears and I am able to make out his features. There is an urgency to his actions as he touches my face and neck with feather-light fingers, his eyes franticly searching for something.

A few moments later he must find it, because I see his body physically relax. Out of the corner of my eye I can see movement happening around me but I don't see who or what it is, I can only see Duncan. *My saviour, my forever songbird. I cannot believe how much he has come to mean to me in such a short time.* After about a minute or two I begin to regain my senses, my hearing is starting to return and it dawns on me that I didn't fully lose my sight this time. *I wonder if it's because of Duncan's touch.* Blinking a few times to clear the remaining fog from my brain, I feel almost back to normal as I slowly sit upright.

"Are you ok? You scared the shit out of me when you collapsed." He asks, a lingering fear present in his voice.

"Sorry, I should have warned you about the side effects of using that ability... and yeah, I'm ok, thanks... Did I get them all?" I ask as I look around the room, while rubbing my head as my headache starts to fade. All I see are soldiers walking around, nothing more. *How long was I down for?* Everyone seems to have recovered from the shock of the attack and are now either attending the wounded or searching the perimeter. I assume it was for more than a couple of minutes. "...Have we found Willow yet?" I ask hopefully.

"We believe you got them all but Damon and his crew are scouring the rest of the tunnels to make sure none escaped or are lurking, waiting to do a sneaky attack while we are recovering. And unfortunately no, we haven't found her yet, they're searching the tunnels for her as well... Do you collapse like that every time you use too much power?" he asks this worriedly as he raises his hand and moves a strand of hair out of my face, placing it behind my ear. The movement and his words make me smile. *He is bothered by this new information and I love that he is being so caring and gentle.*

"For as long as I can remember, yes. I have always collapsed like that. It takes an insane amount of power to do what I just did. Though it didn't last as long this time, usually I am out of it for much longer. I think it may be because you were holding onto me." Lifting my hand, I rest it on the side of his face, needing to feel him. As I touch his warm check, I slide my hand around to cup the back of his head and draw his mouth towards mine. The moment our lips touch I instantly want more and I pull him closer and part my lips so we can deepen the kiss. However, I'm immediately pulling away from his mouth and turning my head to spit out the vile taste that has entered my mouth.

I gaze back at Duncan and see that he is doing the exact same thing I was just doing but in the opposite direction.

"Maybe we should try that another time when we aren't covered in so much shit," He says disgustedly as he turns to spit once more.

"Agreed." I'm laughing as I stand up and I look around to take stock of my surroundings. I need to work off some of this sexual frustration coursing through me and spotting a tunnel leading to the left, I decide I want to check it out. *Maybe I'll find something useful.* I look to Duncan and see that he has moved off to speak with one of the men. He looks to be preoccupied so I decide not to interrupt him and move off towards the passage.

The passageway is small, maybe three people wide and is extremely dark but thankfully because the passage is so small and I'm so bright, I don't need a torch. Making my way further into the darkness, I suddenly glimpse a light coming from around the next corner. Unsure on what I'll find, I raise my blade and holding it against my chest I back up against the wall. I cautiously peer around the corner and see a few of Damon's troops standing off to the far side. Relief washes over me and relaxing my stance, I turn and walk around the corner towards them.

"Did you guys find anything?" I question as my voice breaks into the silence. Startled by my presence, two of the men drop to one knee and aim their bowstrings in my direction. "Whoa, wait guys, it's me," I say as I raise my hands. However, the recognition of my presence doesn't change their stance, they continue to trail their weapons in my direction. *What's going on? They can see me, they know who I am. Why haven't they lowered their weapons?* Without too much movement I slowly make myself battle-ready. Preparing to defend myself if needed. Subtly peering around the men, I try to see what they are standing in front of; they seem to be guarding a door. "What's behind the door guys?" I question casually as if their weapons aren't still aimed at me.

"Never you mind Your Highness. Just turn around and walk away." Says the one with his arrow aimed at my head, the other beside him has the nerve to smirk at me.

"Never you mind? Walk away? I may not be your commander or troop leader, but I am the leader of the light race. So you tell me gentlemen... What's behind the door?" *What in the world is going on? Who do they think they are, talking to me this way? And saying it's none of my business, what a joke!*

"You're right, you're not our leader, nor are you our commander and even though you are the leader of the light race, we still don't have to answer you. Now back the fuck off and walk away before we shoot you."

"Shoot me, are you kidding me?" As the words leave my mouth I take a cautious step forward and as per his word, the soldier fires his weapon but I'm ready. Predicting the attack, I lift my blade and knock the arrow off to the left. The second soldier who's arrow was aimed at my heart, fires and that arrow too gets knocked aside. The three men who had remained standing rush at me with their swords drawn. Not wanting to kill them I make the split second decision to just render them unconscious, long enough for me to see what's behind the door. Moving into a fighting position our swords clash as we move into a deadly dance of limbs and knives, moving left and right.

While defending myself against the three men I rebound off the wall and hit the soldier closest to me on the head with my elbow, knocking him out cold. He falls to the floor as the other two rush towards me to take his place.

Swinging the hilt of my sword into the head of the nearest soldier, he falls back and knocks into the other warrior behind him and takes them both down to the ground.

Luckily, the soldier I hit with my sword accidentally smashes his fist into the other's face upon impact with the floor; and they too are both out cold. *Well, that was easy. Three down, two to go.* Crouched on the ground I look up at the two men who tried to shoot me by the door. "WHAT IS SO IMPORTANT BEYOND THAT DOOR THAT YOU'RE WILLING TO KILL ME FOR IT?" I scream at them in frustration. *In my whole existence I have never seen anyone behave this way. I have never had my own people try to kill me.*

"What's behind this door is nowhere near as important as killing you." The one on the left seethes as the other takes a step closer to me and releases an arrow. This time I am unprepared for the attack and am not quick enough to avoid the arrow that plunges deep into my left thigh, the burning sensation starts almost immediately. Confused for a moment I look down. *That's not a normal arrow. It's an immortal flame arrow!* The intricate celtic swirls are a dead giveaway, they're similar to those on my sun sword. *Where in the world did they get these from? Did the Dark Prince create them?*

Overcoming my shock and pushing my curiosity to the side, I yank the arrow out and quickly lift my head as another arrow is fired. Moving with lightning speed I roll to the side out of its way, my left leg burning with every manoeuvre I make. It appears these men will stop at nothing until I'm dead, so I will just have to do anything necessary to make sure that doesn't happen.

Rushing the men and catching them by surprise I swing my blade and aiming for the asshole on the right, with one clean shot my sword goes straight through his neck. His head making a wet thunk sound as it hits the ground. The second attempts to move out of reach and whirling around I sprint towards him as he tries to flee down the hall but I shoot a quick burst of flame from my hand to block his path. He turns to face me, aiming his last arrow at my heart. Before he has time to release it though, I thrust my blade forward and it pierces his chest. The soldier drops his bow as blood erupts from his wound.

I ignore the mess as I move my face into his and demand, "Who made you these arrows?" The soldier just spits up blood, unable to speak. I watch on with displeasure as the life leaves his body. *Damn! I want to know who the fuck is making weapons that can kill me.* I'm also seriously pissed that I had been left with no other choice but to kill these men. Taking a breath to calm myself I turn to my right and see the door the men were guarding.

Withdrawing my blade from the dead soldier I move cautiously towards it. I reach for the handle and twist it, pulling the door towards me. The wood is so heavy I need two hands to fully open it. As I'm pushing it to open it fully, a light breeze floats out of the room and I'm hit with a familiar scent. *Willow*!

Forgetting my injuries I dash inside and use my power to brighten the room as much as I can. Even with my powers set to high it's still gloomy inside but I search franticly around the space and see a small frame curled up in the corner of the overly large room. My excitement at finding her takes over and without thought I'm running over and I drop to my knees before her. She has her knees up and her head is resting on her legs. What look to be heavy chains are on her ankles and wrists and it appears like she might have something tied around her mouth. *It's her, I've found her*!

Placing my sword on the ground beside me, I whisper as quietly as I can, so I don't startle her, "Willow it's me, I'm here to get you out." I start to untie the knot at the back of her head. It takes a moment but Willow slowly moves from her curled up position and delicately lifts her head just as I finish untying the knot. I get a brief glimpse of eyes that remind me of home and love, before they bug out. Her eyes have shifted to stare at something behind me. Waves of dread are pouring out of her as she stares at whatever it is over my shoulder, I turn my head slightly to see what she is looking at and witness Damon rushing towards me. I have no time to react as he plunges a fire sword deep into my chest.

TO BE CONTINUED...

Acknowledgements

Firstly, I would like to say a huge thank you to my Husband Robby. If it wasn't for you babe, I don't think I would ever have had the courage to get this far, so, thank you. x

Secondly, I would like to thank my mother, Cindy and my sister Loz for proof-reading my book before publication. You will never understand just how nervous I was for you both to read it but I am so glad you did. Your fantastic ideas and contributions helped bring my dream to life and no amount of words will ever be able to portray how much that means to me. So thank you, both of you. x

I would also like to say a huge thank you to my awesome mother-in-law, Alex for designing my wicked cover. You dealt with all my weird and wacky ideas and managed to come up with something really awesome. So very talented, thankyou x

And last but not least, thank you for reading my very first book. I really hope you enjoy it and look forward to finding out what happens in part 2. It means the world to me to know that someone out there will love my characters and story as much as I do.

Always and Forever

Kristen

Follow Me

I would love to hear from you!

You would seriously make my day if you got in contact
with me on my social media pages.

You can find me on Facebook – Author Kristen Dovnik.
I'm on here quiet regularly.

I'm also on Instagram – authorkristendovnik
I'm frequently on here.

And for those of you who do not have social media you can
find me at my website. www.kristendovnik.com

I hope to hear from you soon
X